The Faustian C‍

EXORCIST DANCE
The immortal Toji Kujo has long desired to remake
this world, to burn it down and create peace through
conformity from the ashes. With the most experienced
Exorcists distracted by their showdown with a powerful
demon king, it's up to a Kyoko and a team of young
Exorcists in training to use what they know and hold Kujo
off until help arrives.

ADELAIDE GOURMET
Feast and fuel yourself, the battles and exterminations on
the streets never end. Maya and Colt work on a clean-up
team, their ceaseless task to keep citizens oblivious to
the destruction left in the wake of the immortals. When
some of that mess starts to fight back, they are forced to
confront their own morality and mortality.

RACHEL WALKER AND THE MECHANISM OF TRUTH
After the sudden loss of her best friend, Rachel can't
shake the sense of an ominous presence lingering around
their school. Shadows fill the hallways, and as a student
leader she feels compelled to unmask this threat to her
peers. The unravelling mystery and hidden truths she
unwittingly discovers devastates any sense of certainty in
a world she thought she knew.

EXORCIST DANCE: VERSE OF THE REVOLUTION
Not satisfied, Kujo returns.

ISBN (PAPERBACK): 978-1-922314-11-6
ISBN (EBOOK): 978-1-922314-12-3

Cover art and book design by Andrew Crooks.

Editing by Cameron Rutherford.

Typeset in OpenDyslexic, a new font specially designed to
increase readablity for readers with dyslexia.

Buon-Cattivi Press operates on the land of the Kaurna
people. We pay our respects to elders past and present. We acknowledge
that sovereignty was never ceded, and recognise and respect their ongoing
cultural heritage, beliefs, and relationship with the land.

THE FAUSTIAN CURIOSITY NOVELLAS

ADEN BURG

Buon-Cattivi Press
Adelaide, Australia

For my family and friends, who make
my world of make-believe possible.

Acknowledgements

I would like to start by acknowledging my parents, Daniel and Sharon, who always encouraged me and my path to writing. Along with my little sister, Holly, for being there and not disowning her embarrassing big brother.

I want to acknowledge my lifelong friend, Daniel E, for sticking by a fool like me for so long. Much like how I am grateful for my high school friends Sam, Jayden, Bradley, Zac and Kane for pushing me forward and sticking with me for over ten years now. In much the same way, I want to thank the friends I have made as an adult: Nic, Shiryu, Huckle, Brad, Kenny, Asuka, Neil, Raymond, Tomomi and Yoshiki for expanding my world and encouraging my work.

I am also grateful for the work of Dr Alex Dunkin over the last four years or so, without his patience and guidance, this book would have never taken place. Along with Dr Amelia Walker, who gave me an opportunity and directed me toward this path in the first place. Furthermore, I must acknowledge the University of South Australia's CCRWC and its members Anneliese, Chloe, Dante, Lyndal, Evan, Belinda, Heather, Lily, Eugene, and Simon for their encouragement and allowing me to hear their stories and share my own, from which these stories came to be.

Lastly, I want to acknowledge and thank Kubo-sensei, Kato-sensei, Akutami-sensei, Fujimoto-sensei, Nightow-sensei, Hoshino-sensei, Kadono-sensei, Takei-sensei, Sorachi-sensei and Togashi-sensei, for your amazing worlds and stories that gave me the inspiration and starting for me as a person and as a writer.

Contents

Introduction

In ancient times, demons, creatures born from negative energy, preyed upon humans. The gods of old and their angels merely watched the carnage. Then, 2,000 years ago a redeemer struck down the old gods and assumed authority of the world as the Administrator. He granted select humans, called Exorcists, unique powers to destroy the demons. After 1,800 years, two immortal Exorcists, Toji Kujo and his friend Fraulein Faust, gathered Exorcists who shared their goal. Toji Kujo promoted unity and scouted the strongest Exorcists. The absolute strongest of those were ranked as Paladins in the Exorcist Order. Fraulein Faust created supernatural beings of great power and weapons that could cut down even the immortal. Faust could do nothing but watch as her creations fell into the hands of humans, into their cruelty and their hope. Two hundred years later, the average human can no longer see demons. Instead, the Exorcists rage a quiet and eternal war against demon-kind. Kujo, eager for greater control and authority, seeks to re-order their world by usurping the Administrator. Only a small band of young Exorcists stand against Kujo to maintain the world's order and save countless lives.

EXORCIST DANCE: VERSE OF ADELAIDE

Chapter 0: For Myself, 2000 Years From Now

The girl stared up at the being before her, a woman bathed in light. Six majestic dove wings wrapped around her bare body, which was illuminated by the halo above her head. The woman smiled back at the girl, her emerald eyes meeting the girl's gaze.

'My, my, you can look into my eyes without any fear or reverence. You are quite the interesting one, girl,' the woman remarked through a chuckle.

'Well, this is also interesting for me.' The girl continued to stare.

'Interesting for you as well? Are you not afraid of my presence, confused by its nature?'

'I have never seen an angel before. This is fascinating...'

'Then tell me, what would you do if I was a demon?'

'Demons are real, too? Honestly? I thought they were tales meant to scare bad children.'

'Demons are born from fear and hatred of human beings. Think of them as humanity's shadow, one that will stalk humanity and hunt it in the night.'

'I see! How fascinating.'

'Most humans would be frozen in fear, yet you not only maintain my gaze, but are excited by the notion of demons. You are an amusing human. You will be greatly entertaining to watch. As a reward, I shall grant you one wish.'

'Truly?'

'Of course. Do you think I am not capable? I am a being you cannot comprehend and yet you question me. More than before, I swear I will grant you a wish, for I am certain it will be suitably entertaining.'

'In that case... Please, give me eternal life so I might see days long beyond my own.'

Excerpt from A History of Exorcism by Vial Scriber, 1975

Before the Global Exorcist Order, Exorcists tended to keep to their own nations, people, or homes. However, across history, there have been extinction events that led Exorcists to unite. Exorcists of the Middle East formed a coalition in 1085 after Ishtar incarnated into a demon king. In 1232, the various groups of Exorcists across the African continent formed an alliance in response to the appearance of a Grootslang. The Exorcists of Europe formed a European Exorcist Order in 1648 to counterattack the famine and death wrought by Demon King Pazuzu. However, whilst these examples were all important to the Exorcist Order's eventual formation, none of them were global collaborations.

It was the appearance of Fraulein Faust, one of the major players of the aforementioned 1648 treaty, and Japanese Exorcist Toji Kujo in 1839 that led to a united global Exorcist Order. These two Exorcists brought forward the possibility of an international order that worked together to eradicate demons on a scale never seen before. At this point, the industrial revolution was beginning and the world was becoming far more connected than it had ever been before. To the European Order, the prospect of powerful rein-forcements was one too great to refuse. Hence, they approved the proposal and set about connecting the Order globally. This effort was completed in 1871, with the Order being truly connected with most nations. To better organise the Exorcists, the Order established the Paladins, a group made of the strongest Exorcists worldwide, Fraulein Faust and Toji Kujo being the first of which. Basic tenets were also established after a month of debate between all nations involved, as well as the establishment of clear branches that protected specific geographic areas such as cities or towns. Joint inter-training and exchange programs were established to encourage cooperation between branches.

As a result of all this, demon-related deaths dropped drastically over the next hundred years and demon exorcism rates skyrocketed. The effectiveness of this global collaboration is evident and cannot be overstated.

CHAPTER 1: VS EXORCISTS/FIRE DEMON

05/04/2035 10:15 PM

'The Exorcists evacuated the CBD infuriatingly fast,' the tall woman said before she whistled. Her dangerously vivid hazel eyes gazed into the abyss of the night. She strutted back and forth, her long black shirt and jeans rustling with each exaggerated step. Her crimson hair and sickly pale skin gave her steps a certain fragility, in contrast to the way she licked her lips like a predator anticipating a good hunt.

'Of course they did. They would certainly take my threats seriously. After all, they want to kill me more than anything,' a man replied with a thin smile on his lips. His dark, long hair was tied into a ponytail, which flapped in tandem with the old-world kamishimo he wore. The man leaned against the skyscraper railing. His body possessed the stillness of a marble sculpture as he looked out at the quiet city from this dizzying height.

'Yeah, I guess they have been chasing you for a decade now, Kujo. But I was hoping I'd get to kill some civilians too... Damn, why did you ruin it?' the woman said with a long sigh.

'Now, now, our objective comes first. If we win this

you can kill all you want afterward, Yelena.'

'That is true...'

'Besides, there's going to be someone here you've been wanting to kill for a little while now.'

'For real? She's going to be here?'

'That was a quick change in attitude. Yes, she will unmistakably be here,' Kujo chuckled.

'How do you know that? Are you just manipulating me?' Yelena gave Kujo a sharp glare.

'Demons are ancient creatures born from the negative energy of living human beings. Exorcists are those few humans who are born with the ability to manipulate that negative energy—'

'Yes, yes, we all know this. Is there a point to all this exposition?'

Kujo snickered. 'Of course there is, just be patient.'

'No, hurry up and get to the point.'

'Youth these days, honestly, no respect. My point is each human that possesses negative energy has a distinctly different energy signature, since their energy reflects them as a person. Over the centuries, I have refined my abilities and devised a way to observe these signatures over the distance of one kilometre. Just fifteen minutes ago, nine Exorcist signatures entered my range. Erica Holt, Veronica Kurlu and Ethan Johnson from the Adelaide branch, Julie Vance from the Los Angeles branch, Jacob Jillstone from the New York branch, Atuy Honjo from the Hokkaido branch, Mikoto Shinatobe from the Kyoto branch, Yuya Kitagawa and—of course—Kyoko Nakamura from the Tokyo branch.' Kujo smirked.

Yelena was silent. She stared at her palm and the scar upon it, laced with sentiment toward Kyoko Nakamura. Yelena smiled, exposing all her teeth in a bestial jeer.

'Now I'm invested, can you tell me where she is?'

'Of course, but you might want to hurry. It appears one of our fodder is engaging her as we speak,' Kujo taunted.

'Nah, she'll be fine. No one that has my interest would be weak enough to lose to a small fry. Besides, it's more fun to go at your own pace.' Yelena chuckled as she sprung onto the railing and leapt into the darkness of night. Kujo smirked. Kujo clasped his hands together and closed his eyes. They held shut as the sounds of battle filled the streets below.

05/04/2035 10:17 PM

Kyoko faced the being before her, a humanoid with fire stretching out its head in place of hair. In contrast, Kyoko's lacquered hair neatly stood at her shoulders. Behind a pair of circular glasses, her dark eyes were set on her opponent. Her black track jacket with white stripes on the sleeves swished softly as Kyoko calmly reached for the sheathed katana at her waist. Kyoko was ready to swiftly draw the blade in an instant and slice her enemy into pieces. Across from her the opponent sneered and laughed at her.

'So you're the one Kujo told me about? The Nakamura girl that has Faust's Black Blade? How disappointing. You have barely any negative energy. What was Kujo thinking? You're so weak!' The demon cackled.

Kyoko did not flinch, nor feel insulted in the slightest. In fact, she slowed her breath.

I am strong. I'll let everyone look down on me. I'll accept it all as I destroy the ones who dare to hurt my dear friends.

A smile fell upon Kyoko's lips.

That's right, I don't need to prove anything to those who scorn me. The trust and companionship of my friends, the words of thanks from those that I save, that acknowledgement is enough. I don't need everyone to accept me. It doesn't matter what my family or enemies think. All that matters is protecting my friends. That's enough for me.

Kyoko chuckled.

'You're laughing at me? You stupid, worthless human. Die!' the demon bellowed. It raised its arms.

Kyoko rushed forward with her blade still sheathed. Bullets of flame shot from the demon's arms. Kyoko gracefully weaved between them until she was within arm's reach of the demon. Her blade hissed as she swiftly drew it. The Black Blade shimmered in the moonlight as it swung through the air. After the blade finished its arc, Kyoko skidded to the ground behind the demon.

'Was that your best?' The demon cackled as it turned to Kyoko and raised its arms again. Only for it to be left in stunned silence as its arms fell from its elbows. Blood spurted from its arms. Kyoko moved in and lopped the demon's head off with a gush of fiery blood. The head rolled to the ground and the headless body slumped forward. Kyoko flicked the blood off her blade and neatly sheathed it.

Thanks, Yuya... I should hurry, I need to find the others and—

Kyoko froze at the sound of clapping behind her. She turned to find Yelena seated upon a bench. Kyoko's grip on the Black Blade tightened.

'Nice job. I knew that weakling had no chance, but it was still pleasurable to watch,' Yelena remarked.

Heat pumped through Kyoko's body. Her muscles tensed and she recalled Julie lying on the ground, blood pooling from a small, but deep hole in her chest.

Julie sucked desperate urgent breaths, while Yelena stood above her. Yelena's right hand was caked in Julie's blood. A vicious smile sat on her face.

'I will kill you.' Kyoko's words came from deep in her gut. She drew her blade and pointed it toward Yelena, a vow both to Yelena and to herself. A vow to her previous weaker self that she would not fail again, and that Kyoko would not allow Yelena to hurt or kill anyone again. Yelena chuckled heartily, a child-like smile upon her face.

'Great! You've got the right idea. Then let's do it. Let's have a merry battle to the death. Don't disappoint me now, Kyoko Nakamura!'

Dance

Humans, so contradictorily moral
Demons, so foolishly driven to impulse
I have the stage
Now, please dance
Dance, dance, dance
Dance you foolish creatures,
Dance within my palm
Dance on until the finale,
Until I lower the curtain on this façade of a world

Protect

I won't hesitate
I won't stop
I won't fail
Right here, right now
I will protect them
I won't fail again
I won't falter again

This time,
I will kill you

The Doctrine of the Exorcist Order, 1871

An Exorcist must dedicate themself to destroying demons and protecting people who cannot perceive demons. Only a fraction of people can perceive demons, hence, an Exorcist must honour, value and fight alongside their comrades. This is the way of an Exorcist. Any who turn their blades against those they have sworn to protect or on their comrades are traitors. Traitors of the Order are subject to immediate execution. Even Exorcists who are not members of the Order are to be cut down should their blades be turned upon the Order or the masses.

Chapter 2: Vs Needle Man

Ethan, Jacob and Yuya stood about an empty outer Adelaide suburb. They waited at the street corner, a pedestrian crossing blinking red endlessly. Ethan zipped up his black coat, jostling the assault rifle strapped to his back. Jacob's bright red sneakers squeaked as he stretched enthusiastically. He flicked the hood of his black jacket down, his stylish dreads shining under the moonlight as he hummed an infectious tune. Yuya retied the black belt securing his plain black karate gi. A frown was on his lips as he wordlessly gazed down at his neat brown shoes. Ethan peered at Yuya's frown. Jacob stopped humming, moved to Yuya and put his hand on his shoulder.

'Don't worry. Kyoko will be fine. Remember that joint training event Caroline put us through the first time we all met? Who won that?' asked Ethan.

'Kyoko...' Yuya hesitantly answered.

'Exactly. Kyoko is the strongest Exorcist I know,' said Jacob with a calm smile. 'I mean, I was the strongest guy in my branch. I got a big head from that, but then she comes along and kicks my arse without even trying. That humble pie made me shape up. So, I know she'll be fine on her own, but if she has trouble, we'll just back her up.' Yuya turned to Jacob, his frown still present.

'But I'm worried that she won't even accept our help, that she'll focus on just protecting us. And then she'll—'

'Yuya, do not underestimate Master Caroline or Kyoko,' said Ethan.

'I wasn't, I just—'

'No, you were. Kyoko is strong, but she is also a thoughtful person. I have only known her a short time—perhaps she was different in the past—but if it wasn't for her, I would have submitted to the darkness. She reached out and became my friend. She won't turn us away. Master Caroline knows that too. That's why she assigned us to hunt demons and rendezvous with Kyoko,' said Ethan. A tiny smile shone on his face.

'You have a good point, but I've known Kyoko since we were kids and she's... Well, I'm just worried,' Yuya said in a near whisper.

'Hey, man, you really haven't noticed? Kyoko has changed so damn much. I mean, I've only known her for a little while too. Even then, I noticed during the mock battle, she went at it alone, but these days she's always going about things with all of us. Asking for advice, training with us, even going on missions with us. So, relax, man. She's changed,' Jacob said, giving a thumbs up and a broad smile. Yuya took a deep exhale. His face smoothed out.

'Sorry. Thanks for that, guys,' said Yuya.

'No problem,' said Ethan.

'Actually, if you want, you could even call Kyoko. Maybe she could use a pep talk,' Jacob suggested.

'I-I guess so. Hold on.' Yuya pulled his phone from his pocket and dialled Kyoko.

'Hello, Yuya. Is something wrong?' Kyoko's voice came through.

'She picked up on it right away. Maybe Yuya should be less worried,' Jacob whispered with a grin. Yuya shot Jacob a glare.

'No, I just wanted to talk to you. Is that ok?'

'What did you want to talk about?'

'Well, I just wanted to say, if you get in trouble, you can count on us.'

'Naturally! I trust you all with my life and the same is true for you. I'll rescue you if you get into a pinch. I promise.'

'Thank you. Sorry if it was a little silly. I just had to say that.'

'No, it's not silly. It's good hearing that.'

'Kyoko, you really are the strongest person I know. You *are* strong. You should let all those morons under-estimate you, then utterly crush them,' Yuya chimed in. Yuya was still smiling when he ended the call. He stared at the phone.

'Sounds affirming, see? Nothing to worry about, Yuya,' Ethan finally declared.

'Yeah. Good suggestion, Jacob.'

'Well, you know me. I'm a people pleaser,' Jacob laughed. The others joined in, filling the air with a joy that would soon be drowned out by battle.

05/04/2035 10:16 PM

Ethan, Jacob and Yuya ran down the empty streets, rushing to Kyoko. The pistol in the holster on Ethan's hip jingled and shook as he ran. Jacob smiled as he bounded through the night. Yuya focused only on what was ahead of him, his black karate gi rustling quietly as it swayed ever so slightly with Yuya's controlled run.

The three sensed a presence closing in on them. It trailed behind them. Bloodlust oozed from its presence. Ethan acted first. He raised his assault rifle and let off three quick bursts. Silence followed until a young man stepped out of the shadows, his spiky pink hair and body piercings catching the glow of the streetlights.

'Well, you found me out. I guess that's not a bad thing. That just means I can kill you three, right here and now.' The man licked his lips and straightened his red jacket. Yuya took a deep breath. Jacob tremored.

'Hey, that's a person, right? Apart from Yelena, there were only supposed to be demons in the city, right? So why is a person threatening us? Do we have to fight him?' Jacob gulped.

Damn, they're hesitating. I can't let them fight him. I have to do this, I can't let the others become killers like me.

Ethan thought as he exhaled. 'Leave him to me. Keep going,' Ethan commanded as he raised his assault rifle once more.

'But—'

'Kyoko needs you! Go!' Ethan roared. He let a barrage of bullets loose at the man, who simply chuckled as he effortlessly evaded them.

Yuya and Jacob shared a glance, then ran.

Good. I can take care of this guy. I'm the only one who can do this. But I can't take too long. After I turn this guy into worm food, I'll need to hurry and catch up.

Ethan replaced the emptied clip in his assault rifle. Several translucent white acupuncture needles flew through the air and pierced his right thigh. Ethan kneeled and whined, but he did not stop. He raised his assault rifle and fired until the clip ran empty. Again, the man dodged the bullets with ease. The man sighed, conjured a dozen needles above his fingertip and fired them into Ethan's shoulders. Ethan gritted his teeth as he reloaded again.

I gotta endure this. I have to hurry up and kill him. I need to end this fast.

'Seriously? You're still trying to win? You can't beat me. I'm way faster than your bullets. You should never have tried to fight me. We're a bad match.' The man's needles pierced Ethan's left arm.

Ethan only smiled.

'You're wrong. We're the best possible match,' said Ethan, emptying another clip, only for the man to thrust needles all across Ethan's chest.

Ethan fell onto his back, dropping his assault rifle. His breathing grew heavy. However, Ethan had not given up. He raised his right arm.

That's right... I'm a good match for this bastard. After all, I've actually killed people. These friends of mine... They gave me a world of light... So I have to protect it... I have to make sure that the others aren't exposed to the darkness. They're all fools who hesitate before killing. So, I'll take that on. I'll make sure their light doesn't fade! I'll kill so they don't have to!

Ethan made the shape of a gun with his fingers.

'You're much stronger than I thought... So I have to use everything I have... This is... my strongest technique... Absolute Death: Bullet Magnet!' Ethan fired his finger gun. An immense amount of negative energy scattered out of Ethan, a deep purple mass that enveloped all the bullets Ethan shot and missed. All the bullets turned and drew to his opponent. There was no time for the man to evade nor defend, he was simply reduced to a puddle of blood, flesh and organs. The needles stabbed into Ethan faded into nothing as he struggled to his feet, but he fell back exhausted.

'No... I need to move!' Ethan drew the pistol at his side and fought to stand, but to no avail.

'I can't let them... See it... That's my responsibility... I have to... Kill Yelena... So they don't...'

Ethan's tight grip on the pistol loosened as he fell into a deep slumber. He would not wake until long after the battle had concluded.

My World

Heads with brains oozing out
Guts sprawled everywhere
Final desperate pleads for life
An eternal expression on the corpse
An emptiness within
That is my world
That is what my world left me with
Everyone,
I don't want you all to see that
I don't want you all left with remorse
Please, don't kill
I'll kill for you all, so please
Don't enter my world
Don't leave yourselves with all that pain

Excerpt from *The Definitive Guide to Demons* by Kyle Nines, 1985

Despite centuries of study, there is still no way to permanently wipe out demons. This is because demons are born from ideas filled with fear, hatred and sorrow, which produce negative energy that brings these conceptual beings into existence. As a result, some demons are intrinsically weak, given that they are born from weak concepts like hay fever, whilst others are powerful beings born from concepts like natural disasters. The strongest demons are called demon kings, of which there have been twenty-eight in recorded history and there will be more as the world continues to face many crises.

What this means is that demons and humans are linked, with demons only being able to exist because of human beings. In other words, the only way for human beings to be rid of demons is to first rid the world of themselves. This is precisely why the Exorcist Order is so fundamental in the preservation of the world, as the battle against demon-kind will persist so long as human beings exist. To break such a connection would require the power of the Administrator, and so it is a feat that not even the strongest Exorcist could achieve.

Chapter 3: Vs Bell Demon

05/04/2035 9:30 PM

'Julie, are you afraid?' Atuy asked as he sat upon the muted wooden bench. He flicked his gaze to Julie, adjusting his thick rectangular glasses.

'Y-yeah, I-I-I am. Sorry,' Julie stuttered as she slowly walked to Atuy. Her plaited blonde hair and the black ribbon on her jacket bounced from side to side with her nervous shaking.

'What are you afraid of?'

'Huh?'

'Right now, I'm scared that I'm going to die here. That tonight, I will leave this world in a place far from my home. Veronica, how about you?'

Veronica leaned back on the park bench, her long loose hair and black cloak fluttered in the wind. 'I'm scared that I'll never get to see the sun again, that I'll just be a pile of dust.'

'We're both afraid of dying, but I don't think it's the same for you. Am I right?'

'I'm scared that one of you will die, that I'll be useless again and that someone else will be hurt because of me,' Julie whispered.

'Then, won't you let us be afraid for you? That way, we'll fight hard to protect you and you can protect us. Is that okay with you?' Atuy smiled softly.

'Don't. If I die it'd be better for you.'

'What the hell are you saying? Do you hear what's coming out of your mouth? Do you really blame yourself for what happened with Yelena? That wasn't your fault. You were the one who ended up being hurt, but you hate yourself because someone else fought for you. You don't understand what that even means, but you stand here and say it's better if you die. You piss me off sometimes, you know that?' Veronica stepped up from the bench and marched up to Julie.

'S-sorry.' Julie lowered her gaze to the ground. Veronica grasped Julie's ribbon and pulled her close to Veronica's face.

'Don't apologise. Stop apologising for everything.'

'Okay, Veronica. That's enough,' Atuy said as he shot to his feet.

'Just wait a minute, Atuy. Julie, even if you don't put any value in your life, I do. You're my friend and I want to see a smile on your stupid little face. You're hard-working, clumsy and the kindest person I've ever met, but you can't even see it because you're blinded by your negativity. Everyone else can see it. That's why we'd all be sad if you died. That's why Kyoko fought so hard against Yelena. So don't you ever say that again, got it? If you do, you better grit those teeth.' Veronica released Julie's ribbon. Julie stumbled backward and blinked heavily.

'Well said, Veronica. I concur,' Atuy said softly.

Julie swallowed. 'I'll do my best,' she squeaked.

'That's the spirit! I believe in you as always. So believe in me and all the others who believe in you.' Veronica grinned.

'The same is true for me,' Atuy added with a nod.

'Thank you. I'll be counting on you two as well,' said Julie, her voice and expression firm.

05/04/2035 10:20 PM

Julie's ocean-blue eyes shot open as she stood. She grasped her heart through her jacket and her legs trembled. Julie took in a deep breath and steadied herself.

'A powerful demon is here. Please be careful,' Julie breathed.

Atuy flicked his glasses. His sharp eyes were steeled.

'Of course,' he replied as he pushed back his spikey dark hair.

'Yeah, we'll win for sure,' said Veronica. Her long hair bobbed as she stepped forward with a clack of her heeled boots and a swish of her long flowing black cloak.

A voice chuckled and bells rang out. They turned to see a demon, whose body slowly appeared more and more with each toll of the bell. It was a woman in a blue kimono with horns upon her head and streaks of red in her white hair. She carried two large bells attached to cloth. The bells clanged against each other, ringing out harshly with a reverberating echo of steel.

'You found me already, huh? Well, I guess that's good. Now I don't have to wait to kill you. I'm Rin. The ringing of the bells is how you'll die, humans.' Rin licked her lips at her weak prey. Julie took in another deep breath.

'You'll be the one dying, demon. Now, I beseech you, help me, guardian spirit!' Atuy raised his right palm and extended it to his right shoulder. Negative energy flowed out of it and a large bipedal creature appeared behind him. The creature lunged at Rin, ready to ram with monstrous horns and claw with long fingernails. Rin simply chuckled and flicked the large cloth she carried. One of the bells rang. The sound resonated and stopped the roaring creature in its tracks.

'I see. You turn sounds into attacks with those bells. Easy, we'll have this done in a flash.' Atuy smirked. Julie tightened her fists and nodded.

'You're a little too slow for this, but my technique is fast enough. I'm taking this one,' Veronica declared with a clap of her hands. Julie understood Veronica's intention at once.

Atuy's guardian spirit is incredibly fast, but she's trying to mislead the enemy. That way, Atuy can swoop in with the deciding blow.

'Alright then, come here, Julie. We'll watch as Veronica takes care of this weakling.' Atuy smiled as he sat crossed-legged upon the ground. Julie rushed to his side.

Atuy's acting too. He wants the demon to drop her guard and ignore him. While that happens, I'll use my sensory technique to hide his negative energy. It'll give Atuy an opportunity to gather negative energy and unleash a powerful surprise attack. Alright, I need to focus! We can do this!

'You cocky brats!' Rin screamed as she wildly rattled the bells. Ringing attacks echoed rapidly toward Veronica, who opened her palms to reveal a bright flame.

'Land's Healer: Purifying Flame!' Veronica called as the flame spurred a barrage of fireballs. As the fireballs and soundwaves of the bells touched, they negated each other with a fizzle.

'Well now, our attacks cancel each other out. I guess the winner will be the one who can break through, which means you're screwed,' said Veronica. She let another fireball barrage loose. Ringing echoes and blazing balls of ember clashed between the two women.

Despite all that chaos and noise, Julie focused on using her technique to conceal Atuy's negative energy. Through her focus, the concentration of her feelings, her past seeped in negativity bubbled to the surface. Julie recalled being hated due to the circumstances of her birth. She recalled being looked down upon by all the other Exorcists around her for her weak technique, a sensory type that could only accurately detect or hide negative energy within four hundred metres of herself. She was called a contradiction, a waste of space, because despite her boundless pool of negative energy, she couldn't even fight.

I used to think me being small and timid was fitting. That if I disappeared, the world would be a better place. But these people, they see me as their valuable ally. They make me... Determined to live and to win. I won't back down or run away. Even if I can only support them, I'll do my damn best. Even if my body is small, my soul is large when I'm with them.

'Now,' Atuy whispered. Julie dodged out of the way of Atuy's guardian spirit. It bounded behind Rin and seized her bells.

'Can't do anything without these, can you?' Atuy smirked as he watched Rin struggle to no avail. The guardian had her locked in place.

'Land's Healer: Rejuvenation Cycle,' Veronica called out. The flame in her hands shifted into a circular wheel. It flung out of Veronica's hands, hurtled toward Rin and cut her into two clean halves. Julie let out a large breath and leaned forward.

We did it! We won!

'Good job! That was a spectacular attack,' said Atuy.

'Thanks, but the support from you guys was the true star of this battle.'

'Yeah, great job, Atuy.'

'What are you talking about Julie? Your technique is what allowed me to attack. Take some credit for yourself. You certainly deserve it,' said Atuy. He shifted up his glasses with his right index finger.

'Yeah, be proud,' said Veronica, batting her playfully.

I'm wanted... They think I should be proud? Just for using my useless technique? Just for being there? For being me? It's hard. I don't get it... It's nice...

'Thank you,' was what she finally squeaked out.

Julie wasn't able to enjoy her praise for very long. A deathly chill ran down her spine. A presence appeared and started to move towards them from their right.

'Who is this? How could I not sense them before? How did Kujo ally with a demon like this?' Julie said through sharp breaths. Atuy and Veronica rushed to her side to comfort her with a hand on her each shoulder.

It's so full of malice. The air is so cold. It'll kill us! I... I need to calm down. I can't let my cowardice hurt them.

'Run! If we don't run, we'll—'

'Die? How vulgar. I don't kill humans. Well, at least not the ones I like. So as long as you stay on my good side, you'll be fine,' a voice said from behind them. The trio turned to see a young man wearing a suit, bowtie and top hat.

'Ah, I'd best introduce myself,' said the man. He removed his top hat and bowed, revealing white hair and neat little horns upon his head.

'My name is Samael. Humans have called me the demon king of time. It is a pleasure to make your acquaintance.' Samael smiled warmly, yet the three humans were silent, fearful.

This demon is in an entirely different league. He's close to being a god. Even so... If we can't escape, then I won't let this demon hurt Atuy and Veronica.

Julie stepped forward.

'We won't lose, even to you,' she declared, her fist in balls, every part of her screaming.

Thank You

Feared, from when I was born
Hated, from when my technique appeared
Looked down upon, whenever I try
So, thank you
Thank you for trusting me
Thank you
Beyond words,
I thank you

Excerpt from *The Master and Student Odyssey* by Adam Dakota, 2042

Despite the Exorcist Order's insistence on cooperation and understanding, there are still plenty of Exorcists who are discriminated against. It is only natural that the techniques, fighting styles and beliefs of some Exorcists, are considered taboo by others. In addition, a fair number of Exorcist communities and families hold onto not only their techniques, but the centuries-old values that follow them. As such, many of these communities and families discriminate against others because they still hold onto narrow worldviews about life, women, childbirth and love. Discrimination is inevitable because Exorcists are human beings, just like the ordinary people they protect. Consider the socio-political environment at the time of the Order's foundation: rampant imperialism, genocide, racial discrimination and the denial of women's rights in most countries to name a few issues. Do you honestly think that just because these people had a shared purpose that they would not discriminate against and hurt each other?

Chapter 4:
Vs Demon King of Time

05/04/2035 9:35 PM

A petite girl in traditional red shrine maiden attire overlooked the city as she sat upon a bed of lush green grass. A calm wind blew through the air and brushed against her cheeks. The girl let out a small sigh as she looked up to the stars.

'It is so beautiful. I thank you, world,' the girl muttered to the wind.

'I feel the same way, Mikoto. This world can be wonderful at times,' Kyoko said.

Mikoto turned to Kyoko, who was sitting underneath a large gumtree with her sword resting on her shoulder.

'Oh, I thought you were on the phone.'

'Just finished.'

'If you do not mind me asking, who was it?'

'Yuya. He always makes me feel stronger,' Kyoko chuckled.

'Ah, he is your childhood friend, is he not?'

'Yeah, the only friend—no—person that I have had in my life for a long time.'

'The only person? No family or mentors?'

'My family all hate me. My mother does not see me as a person, only dead weight. My younger siblings either look down on me or see me as a symbol of shame, except for Yujiro and Keisuke. So, my mother made sure I could never spend time with them. I was banished to a tiny shack, a derelict little building left over from the Edo period, on the edge of our family compound when I was seven. They sent the son of the retainer family to cook my meals and look over me.'

'Was that Yuya? He befriended you on the spot, I take it?'

'To be honest with you, I found it hard to relate with other people. They either laughed at me, or they had happy families, while I suffered. When this cheery boy stepped into my shack with his stupid smile, I punched him square in the face.'

'How horrible!'

'Right? I was a real brat. Yuya really had his work cut out for him, but he befriended me in the end. After all, seeing someone smile at me felt nice for a change.'

'How lovely. Is this what led to the current you?'

'Yes. I was still pretty prissy until the end of middle school. I still thought that, aside from Yuya, I could not fully trust anyone. But because of him, I knew what a friend was and what a good person was. So, when I met you all, I was able to recognise that in all of you. At first, I must admit, I found it hard. Yet, in very little time, I began thinking of you all as my friends,' Kyoko said with a warm smile.

'I see. I can relate. I only had my mother. Everyone else reviled us.'

'For your technique, right?'

'Yes, our technique is not fit for battle nor killing. Hence, the other Exorcists in the Kyoko branch treated my mother as though she were dirt, especially since she had me out of wedlock. I thought everyone else outside of our family was scum.'

'Then, what do you think of us?'

'Well... You are like the siblings I never had. You are my family. From my perspective, everyone else can go to hell,' Mikoto said resolutely.

'Nothing wrong with that, but perhaps in the future we should try to make more connections with other people.'

'Why?'

'Well, it is not good to stay in an isolated box. I would know. We should try to expand our worlds together.'

'That sounds frightening. People can be vicious. We both know that.'

'Yes, but we both took a leap with the others and look at how that turned out. Expanding our worlds made us both better as people.'

'But what if it just causes us pain again?'

'Then, our friends will help us.' Kyoko grinned.

'Kyoko, how are you this strong—no—this incredible?'

'I wouldn't say I'm incredible, just stubborn.'

Mikoto blinked. 'What do you mean?'

'I did normal strength, stamina, reflex, and survival training. But it wasn't the training itself that made me strong.'

'Then what made you strong?'

'My resolve. I just can't bear the thought of giving up, of surrendering. It used to be because of my family, because I had to prove they were wrong about me all on my own. Now it's because I have people I want to protect and stand beside. I simply refuse to give up. I will keep pushing on until I achieve my goal. To protect my friends, I won't ever stop, I won't ever concede or walk away no matter how tough it gets or how much I want to cry. Every time I'm at my breaking point I think, "Never stop. Just keep walking".'

Kyoko's eyes were locked with the silent Mikoto's.

'Ah, sorry,' said Kyoko. 'That was a little intense. Anyway, that's just my own stupid stubbornness. Don't feel like you have to follow my example, alright? There are many paths to strength, with no truly correct path. Just go with what works best with you.'

'No, that's fine.' Mikoto shook her head. 'I rather like your way of doing things.'

'Is that so? Well, do your best then.' Kyoko smirked.

05/04/2035 10:20 PM

Mikoto exhaled multiple short breaths. The metal rings at the head of her staff jingled as Mikoto's grip on the base tightened.

I eliminated ten and yet... There is no end...

Before her were at least twenty or so demons. Their sizes and shapes varied drastically. All of them were monstrous. Their inhuman eyes locked upon Mikoto. They sought to devour the petite girl before them.

The odds appear rather insurmountable this time. I may have to concede death. After all, my battle prowess with a staff may be grand, but I can only go so far without a combat-based technique. My healing technique is completely useless here, as is my sealing technique. I suppose this is the end...

Mikoto loosened her grip on her staff and shut her eyes.

'Never stop. Just keep walking.'

The words burst through Mikoto's mind and forced

her eyes open once more. A smile formed on her lips.

Thank you, Kyoko! I will!

'Come! I will face you all!' Mikoto roared as she raised her staff with renewed vigour.

'That's what I like to hear,' called out a voice from above. 'Let me help. Here's my grand entrance!' Something crashed into the demons with a loud bang that sent out a small shockwave and dust into the air. When the dust cleared, the tall and muscular figure of Erica stood upon the corpses of the demons. Her blond ponytail blew back and her black jacket swayed with the last gust of the shockwave. The oni's face on the back of the jacket appeared to contort in pain as the material wrinkled.

'Amazing...' was all Mikoto could utter.

'Ah, damn.' A look of disappointment burrowed upon Erica's soft yet intimidating face. 'I didn't think that would be so easy... Oh, right. I came to help you. You did great. I love your enthusiasm. It reminds me of my little sis Kyoko. Great job, little sis Mikoto!' Erica smiled broadly.

"Little sis"? How odd. Actually, I do recall Ethan telling me Erica refers to everyone younger than her as siblings. He said it was a weird trait I should ignore. But...

'Thank you, elder sister. I assume we are going to head to provide assistance to Kyoko?' Mikoto gave a polite bow that put her body in a perfect right angle, one that concealed the bright smile upon her face.

How wonderful! I have wanted to call Kyoko and Erica 'elder sister' for some time. I should try calling Kyoko 'elder sister' the next time I see her. Oh, and Jacob as 'elder brother'.

'Of course. Great thinking.' Erica grinned. as she gave Mikoto a thumbs up.

How informal... I love it! She is so cool. Mikoto

chuckled as she thought that. However, she would not be able to relish in the thought, as a wave of deep dark energy fell upon them. It screamed of killing intent and power. Thick and hard to shake, it sent sweat down Mikoto's forehead.

'What is that?'

'Damn. I'll need your help, little sis Mikoto. You have a sealing technique, right?'

'Yes, however, it only works under very specific conditions. My technique forces a demon or person into a vessel. This can only occur with high amounts of negative energy, as the technique's strength cannot perceive lower-level demons and the vessel has to be appropriate, like sacred paper, an object of worship or sometimes even a person. I can't seal a demon into anything.'

'That's perfect. We don't have much time. We need to get moving. I'll explain on the way, trust me,' Erica said.

Mikoto hesitated for a second. However, she found herself unable to walk away from the words of her new elder sister.

'Of course, elder sister!'

05/04/2035 10:21 PM

It all happened in an instant. The demon king Samael stepped forward.

'Hmm, you're interesting. I think I'll save you for last. Time Distillation: 0.01,' Samael declared as he tapped Julie's forehead.

Julie froze in place. Not even her eyes moved.

'What the hell did you do to her?' Veronica called out. She clapped her hands and prepared to unleash hellfire upon Samael.

'Right now, that girl is experiencing the world one one-hundredth of its original speed. Any movement will take an eternity, but don't worry. She will be fine, unlike you.'

Samael blinked from existence for a split second and reappeared before Veronica. She went to attack with her left arm, only for it not to respond. Instead, it sat limp by her side. She would have gasped in shock, were it not for the blood that sprayed from her mouth and the pain roared in her stomach.

'Did I mention I can speed up my own perception of time? My Time Acceleration ability has increased my reaction speed two hundred times faster than normal. For a human, it would be a useless power their body could not keep up with. I have slowed my speech to a crawl so you can understand. See how futile this battle is? You cannot even understand my attacks until the damage is done,' Samael said with a leer.

'That will not stop me!' Atuy rushed in with his guardian spirit.

Samael appeared behind him and yawned.

He's playing with us, thought Veronica. *He explained his technique because he knows we can't do anything about it. He could have already killed us both. I didn't even feel anything. Now I can barely fight and Atuy is being messed with.*

Veronica gritted her teeth and attempted to move. Pain that seared throughout her stomach.

Damn! Come on! Move!

Veronica gasped and struggled to budge in vain.

Move! Move! Move!

'You're still trying? I commend you, human. What drives you so?' Samael smirked, his gaze entirely upon Veronica as he effortlessly dodged Atuy's every attack.

'I don't even need to think about it. I know why I'm willing to die here.'

Veronica grinned as she forced herself to kneel and face Samael.

'It's my bond with the others. I'm putting everything I have into this. Atuy, give me everything you have as well!' Veronica raised her right hand, putting all her negative energy into it. 'Land's Healer: Summer Rebirth!' Veronica roared as a massive wall of flame rushed to Samael.

'Incredible!' Samael smiled as he leapt far above it, a move that Atuy had been waiting for.

'I am Atuy! The sea! That which none can tame or bind.' With that roar, Atuy's guardian spirit slammed its fist into Samael's face and smashed him to the ground. A loud bang echoed, followed by silence.

'Did... we win?' Veronica asked with wide eyes.

'I think so,' Atuy huffed. A smile formed on his panting lips.

'Incredible,' came from Samael's voice. 'You actually managed to hit me. I am impressed. You humans have earned my respect.'

Samael rose to his feet. There were no marks, no wounds where he was hit. There wasn't even any dirt on him.

A deep dark presence full of malice and pure killing intent burned its way into Atuy and Veronica. They fearfully turned to the source.

'Ah, it has been a while since the brat's been weak enough for me to come out. How thrilling,' Julie grinned as she cricked her neck and cracked her knuckles. She took her ribbon to tie her hair into a ponytail and tossed her jacket aside which sailed through the air. It slowly arched down until it landed on Atuy's lap.

'How did she—Huh? What's going on with her eyes?' Atuy gaped.

Julie's eyes had turned green and a massive toothy smile was upon her face. Samael bowed to her.

'I see. Is it truly you, Lady Lucifer? Only one as grand as you could break free from my technique.'

'Yes. It's me. This brat is my vessel in this era. She's a descendant of mine, though she's disappointingly weak and docile. However, she does have an immense amount of negative energy and an interesting sensory technique at her disposal. It makes her body quite entertaining to play in,' Lucifer said with a smirk.

'I am honoured to meet you. As a demon, your very presence in this age honours me.'

'Thanks, thanks. I like you too. You're strong and those who are strong are the ones I love most in this world. So how about it? Are you willing to fight me? I promise it'll be entertaining.'

'Of course, but may I request a condition if I win?'

'That could be amusing. I will vow to honour it if you satisfy me.'

'Then, if I am victorious, please tell me how you incarnated and help me achieve my goal,' Samael pleaded.

'Alright then, sounds great.' Lucifer smiled, and an even greater dark aura pooled out of Julie's body. Atuy and Veronica could only look upon the monster, a true divine being, one untouchable by the hands of humans.

Sister

An only child
Responsible alone
So thank you sister

Soul

Beyond life and death
Linking so much love and vows
Our souls always burn

Excerpt from *Angels: The Black Box of the Old Gods* by Thomas Yoast, 2003

It is a fact that angels exist. The existence of Fraulein Faust and the sealed Angel Of Knowledge validates this fact beyond all measure. Yet, even Fraulein Faust does not know what angels are. She has simply noted that the angels proclaim themselves as the natural opposite of demons. For this reason, many have argued that angels are born from the love of human beings, as opposed to their hatred. However, if this is true, why have no new angels appeared after two millennia? This is because angels are not born human beings, but instead, created by the old gods, which explains why they are the natural opposite of demons. They were created, not born, by their creators, and reflect not negativity, but divinity.

Chapter 5: Vs Lucifer

'Time Acceleration: Ten Thousand Times Acceleration!' Samael roared.

'Nice, nice. I'm going to give you a strong attack then. Spatial Destruction: Reverberation,' Lucifer chuckled.

An immense boom burst through the air. It tore the brick buildings apart, ripped up the concrete street, shattered all the glass from every building and even tore down the skyscrapers that towered far into the sky as though they were paper. It cracked the earth and resounded across the shattered streets. Atuy focused everything he had into his guardian spirit. He gave it all his negative energy.

I won't let us die here. We still have things to do. Dreams to see, friends to walk beside. We can't die. Not yet.

The world seemed to rumble as shockwaves passed over Atuy and Veronica, an event of power and destruction beyond what they could have ever imagined. Atuy's guardian spirit wrapped them up in its arms, just barely managing to protect them.

'I'm out, sorry,' Atuy apologised with a long exhale. His guardian spirit faded into the wavering air.

'What do we do now?' Veronica said.

'I don't know... But we can't give up. We need to—'

Julie's body, piloted by Lucifer floated to the ground. She landed firmly on both feet with a soft tap. In her arms she held the severed torso of Samael. Atuy looked around him. The entire block had been razed. Nothing remained except smoke and chunks of rubble. The mass of buildings that had once stretched into the sky and even the roads had been wiped away.

They caused this much damage in minutes? And only the two of them? They're monsters!

'Thanks for that fight. That was the first time in five hundred years I had to fight for real. I truly enjoyed it.' Lucifer smiled at the severed Samael.

'Thank you... It is... an honour.'

'The truth is, I can't really, truly die. Even if I'm defeated, I'll simply be reborn. After all, I'm not a demon. The true nature of my being is hard to put into terms that can be understood through a human language, but I suppose you can refer to me as an angel for lack of a better description. I was created by the original Administrators of this world, before they were usurped by that interesting boy. We had a great fight, the only fight I have truly lost. After, unable to die but weak and unable to fight, the boy gave me to my human descendants. They sealed me within one of them and they have continued that annoying tradition for about two thousand years or so. See, if my host dies, I also die. Every time that happens, it takes two hundred years for me to reincarnate once more. At that precise moment of rebirth, they seal me in a new host,' Lucifer explained with a smirk.

'My prize... But, I did not win.'

'I never said you had to win. I said you had to satisfy me. You did so splendidly. I will remember this battle forever.'

'Thank you...' Samael smiled, his dead eyes arching upward.

Lucifer gently placed his body on the ground. She kneeled beside him for a moment.

Lucifer stood and looked over to Atuy and Veronica.

'You two are still alive? I wasn't holding back. I thought you would be dead for sure. I'm impressed. I think I'll let you live a while longer. However, my condition is you two must train and come back stronger—'

Erica's fist hurtled toward Lucifer's face, but Lucifer easily caught it in the palm of her hand.

'Sorry, you can't surprise me, Erica. I can use the brat's sensory technique. She's still far too weak in body and spirit to use mine, but I can take full advantage of her oh-so-useful talents,' Lucifer said.

'"Sorry" isn't going to cut it. You put my little brothers and sisters in danger. I'm going to kick your arse.'

'How amusing! You've gotten much stronger since last time too. I'm so glad. Your growth is beautiful. However, you still need to grow more, to get even stronger. Right now, you'd only last thirty seconds against me. So, I'm going to put a hold on that fight. I'll just be on my way.' Lucifer smiled and waved, then went to pass Erica.

'Increased Seal: Cage of the Wailing Beast,' Mikoto proclaimed as she struck the ground with her staff with a loud metallic clang. Green energy surged around Lucifer as she winced.

'Funny, it seems neither of us intended to fight.' Erica smirked. Lucifer's eyebrow twitched as she made eye contact with Mikoto.

'Oh, you're a descendant of Himiko? I should have guessed. You look just like her. You even dress like her. To think that girl is still a pain in my arse, even after all these centuries. I see you're making the seal stronger. Oh well. When I finally manage to come out again, you'll all be magnificently strong.' Lucifer smiled widely, baring her teeth. The dark energy in the air disappeared with a final crackle like thunder. Lucifer cackled before her eyes shut and she fell backward into Erica's arms.

When those eyes reopened, they were the blue eyes of Julie. She gripped the ribbon in her hair and pulled it loose. Her hair flung out. Julie brought her fist to her face and opened it. She stared at the black ribbon. She sobbed, water forming in her eyes as her hand shook and became a fist again. Her lip quivered as she buried her face into her other hand.

'Erica, Mikoto, Veronica, Atuy, I'm sorry. She took advantage of my emotions. She came out because I couldn't calm down. I could see and hear everything, but I was too weak. I couldn't stop her again. I'm sorry. I'm so sorry. Please, kill me.' Tears rolled down Julie's red cheeks. Her wheezing breaths grew short and sharp. Erica softly hugged Julie.

'You didn't choose to have that monster in you. That's not your fault. In this world I don't think very many things can be considered pure good or evil. Lucifer is an exception. She is absolutely evil. Julie, never blame yourself for her actions. However, you have to become strong enough to contain her. Vow to never let this happen again. Contain her successfully next time,' Erica said quietly. Julie turned to Erica and found a radiant smile before her.

'Yeah, and we'll become strong enough to help you,' Atuy added as he walked up to Julie and placed her jacket over her shoulders.

'Right, if that devil shows up again, I'll kick her arse until she apologises to you,' Veronica proclaimed. Julie's eyes welled with tears.

'Thank you,' Julie sobbed. She tightly embraced

Erica.

'Alright, Mikoto, give Atuy and Veronica some first aid. Then we're making a B-line for Kyoko. The three of you should stay here. You guys are in no condition to fight,' Erica said.

'Of course, elder sister, but why? I can heal these two back to full health. Why would I simply provide first aid?'

'I have a bad feeling. I want you to keep most of your negative energy in stock just in case. The appearance of Lucifer can't have been a coincidence. Sorry, it's not concrete evidence, but that's just what my gut is telling me.'

'I agree. This is odd. Think about it. Kujo has the ability to detect all presences within his range. Of the eight of us, the biggest threats to Kujo are Mikoto and Kyoko, the ones who possess the sealing technique and the only weapon that can kill an immortal. So, why did Kujo send a demon king to our group?' Atuy said, wiping his glasses with a cloth he pulled from his back pocket.

'Maybe to eliminate Lucifer?' Veronica suggested. 'No Exorcist alive could defeat that monster. But Kujo is the strongest person in the city, right? It seems Lucifer likes to fight strong enemies. Wouldn't it stand to reason that person would have been Kujo? That seems like something he would definitely want to avoid.'

'That would be a good point, except that Lucifer can only take over my body if I'm too weak physically or emotionally to resist her or if I... if I give her my body...' Julie trembled.

Erica tightened her embrace and Julie let out a slow breath to still her body.

'Basically,' Julie continued, eyes now firm. 'If Kujo wanted to avoid fighting Lucifer, he wouldn't have sent a demon king to put me in a life-or-death position.

Especially since Kujo knew my ancestors quite well. He knows everything about our seal.'

'No wonder it was weird. He wanted Lucifer to appear. But why would he...' Atuy trailed off as he placed his glasses on his face.

'Damn!' Veronica cursed. 'Did we fall into his trap?'

'It doesn't matter. It seems like Kujo is two moves ahead of us. All we can do is move forward and beat him,' Erica said.

'Indeed, that horrid man is absolutely a devilish schemer. We must not let him get his way,' Mikoto said with her brow furrowed.

'Then get going,' Veronica said. 'We'll be fine. You can heal my arm after you save the world. Go get a few hits in for me.'

'Do not relent,' Atuy declared, arms crossed.

'Please, defeat Kujo,' Julie said softly, her hands clasped together.

'Of course. Leave it to us,' Erica said and flexed her right arm.

The Flowers

Flowers live short
Only a brief instant in the expanse of the universe
Only for an instant, do they bloom
And yet,
It is so immensely beautiful
I must see them bloom,
Across the ages
So I can truly enjoy the beauty of the flowers

Excerpt from Toji Kujo's Manifesto, 2034

To most people, demons are fairy tales, something parents tell their children about to make them behave. Unlike us Exorcists, they cannot perceive demons. As such, our world and our struggles are completely invisible to them. No matter how many of us die, no matter how many of us sacrifice our lives, they will never know. In fact, our efforts have not changed anything in the world. Our powers have not affected politics or technology. Especially since the Order forbids the use of techniques for anything except the preservation of life and the slaying of demons. This world is on rails, the carriage hurtling toward a fatal crash our powers could prevent. Instead, we are quietly dying out of sight.

Chapter 6: Vs Yelena

Kyoko swung at Yelena's neck.

'Blood Shield!' Yelena chanted.

Kyoko's blade came to a grinding halt, blocked by a small shield of blood. Kyoko pushed away and swung again.

'Blood Spikes!' Yelena clicked her fingers. Five bright foot-long red spikes extended from her right arm. Yelena smirked and rushed at Kyoko with her right arm brandished.

Kyoko easily sidestepped her and moved to slice Yelena's stomach open.

'Blood Spear!' A short red spear protruded from Yelena's left palm as she tore toward Kyoko, who was left open from her attack.

Backing off, Kyoko blocked the Blood Spear with her blade but the force of the blow sent her skidding backward.

'I thought that would get you, though I'm glad it didn't. This is too thrilling!' Yelena cried.

'Shut up,' Kyoko snarled, trying to focus. This battle was in a stalemate. They were evenly matched and unable to overwhelm one another. The only chance Kyoko had at victory was to get a decisive blow.

I have to do it. No matter what, I have to kill her.

Kyoko focused her calm killing intent and raised her blade in an even stance.

'Alright, enough breaks. Let's keep dancing.' Yelena laughed before she ran full force at Kyoko.

'Chain of Restriction,' Yuya's voice broke through the air. A thick and heavy chain wrapped itself around Yelena's left arm.

'Lightning Strike!' Jacob called as he leapt through the air. The air sizzled around him as his right arm soared toward Yelena's face.

Yelena shot up her right palm and focused shifting her blood outside it. She gritted her teeth as she blocked Jacob's blow.

Kyoko saw her chance and went right for Yelena's neck once more. Kyoko swung. Yelena stepped backward at the very last possible instant, Kyoko's sword just scratched her chin.

'Blood Spears!' Yelena called as multiple large spears protruded through her torso toward Kyoko, who sprang backward to evade the attack. Despite this, Kyoko was smiling.

'Jacob, Yuya, thank you. I managed to finally get a hit because of you two,' Kyoko said. Yuya gave Jacob a sheepish smile. Jacob chuckled.

'Sorry, Jacob, you were right,' Yuya conceded.

'Yeah, see? It's all good.'

'What are you talking about?' Kyoko cocked her head.

'Nothing, just— Um— Well—' Yuya stammered.

'Just about how you'd be fine.' Jacob smirked.

'I'm not sure I understand, but now you're here, I'm better than fine.'

'Alright then, let's beat our enemy together! Jacob and I will create an opening for you. You wait then strike.' Yuya cracked his knuckles.

'You two can do it!' Kyoko cheered.

'Alrighty then. Let's get started.' Jacob's body was enveloped by lightning and disappeared into sizzled air.

'Blood Barricade!' Blood shields and spears appeared all over Yelena's body, except her left arm, still wrapped up in Yuya's chain. Jacob zoomed in and out of her sight. He moved at near god-speed and effortlessly evaded her wild flailing body. Jacob shot to Yelena's left side. Yuya pulled his chains back from Yelena's left arm with a small yank of his right arm. Jacob focused his strength into one powerful strike.

If he succeeds, with that power, Jacob will completely destroy her arm. It's the opening I need. I just have to wait and trust in it. With that thought, Kyoko exhaled and watched, her grip on her sword still tight. Yelena chuckled. A blood spear burrowed out of her left palm toward Jacob.

'Chain Shield!' Yuya's chains wrapped themselves around Jacob's arm.

It's a combination attack. Lightning and metal naturally enhance each other. Their attack is strong enough to break through Yelena's blood. Keep going! You can do it!

Jacob's fist burned through the blood as it made contact. Yelena reeled back as the remaining electricity melted the other blood shields and spears right off Yelena.

Jacob stopped, catching his breath, the lightning dissipated around him. He was out of negative energy. He burnt through all of it to create this one chance for Kyoko to kill Yelena.

Kyoko rushed in, her blade raised above her head.

'How marvellous,' said Yelena. 'I thought more people would disrupt us, my dear Kyoko. You've forced me to use my trump card.' Yelena extended her right hand. 'Complete Blood Focus: One Thousand Needles.'

Thousands of tiny blood needles appeared in the

air and soared toward the three. Yuya used all his negative energy to wrap them in his strongest defensive chains. The chains pulled tight around Kyoko and Jacob.

But he could not create any chains for himself. The needles pierced his body. He fell to the ground in a sputter of blood. Yelena giggled.

'Yuya!' Jacob screamed as he rushed to Yuya. He slid down to kneel beside him. 'He's alive! But he's badly hurt. He might not make it,' Jacob cried.

Kyoko was silent. Her vision fractured. Her breathing quickened.

Yuya is hurt. I... I failed. I have to kill her. I failed. Kill her. I couldn't help them. I was useless again. Kill. Useless. Kill. Useless! KILL!

'DIE!' Kyoko screamed. She went to run toward Yelena, only to be stopped by a hand firmly grasping her shoulder.

'Calm down, Kyoko.' Kyoko turned to see Erica standing behind her, her eyes soft.

'But I have to! Yuya is... Yuya is dying! I just—'

'Listen to elder sister,' Mikoto interjected, placing her hands upon Yuya to heal him. 'Yuya will be fine under my care.'

Thank god, he's safe. But, I...

'Erica... I wasn't able to...' Kyoko's eyes sank to the ground.

'Kyoko, we're Exorcists. We put our lives on the line. Naturally, we get hurt. Sometimes we die. You can't protect us all the time. That's why you have to trust in your comrades and fight with them as equals. Even when they are hurt and fall, you have to trust them and use their resolve to keep fighting. Right, Jacob?'

Jacob grinned. 'Yeah! Before, Yuya protected us not to simply shield us, but to entrust the fight to us.

He had faith we would be able to win without him. I trust you guys can win this. That's why I used all my power. Keep going. Win.'

'See? Now come on, little sis. We must win this.' Erica threw off her jacket. Underneath was a singlet that showed off her muscular build.

Kyoko raised her sword tightly once more. 'Thank you, Erica.'

'Ooh, even more of you,' chimed Yelena. 'I wonder how—'

'You're incredibly annoying.' Erica clicked her tongue before dashing across the ten metres between herself and Yelena and struck her face. Blood sprayed out from Yelena's mouth.

Yelena was forced to step back. Kyoko came for her once again in a sprint. Yelena leapt into the air as Kyoko's blade soared forward. It struck Yelena's thigh and left a bloody cut. Yelena landed with a wince.

We can do this. With Erica here I can win this. Together, this battle is ours. I can kill her. With my trust in the others, I can kill Yelena!

Resolve

Keep walking,
Never stop
Do not waste their sentiments,
Do not disrespect their sacrifices and determination
Just keep on going,
Trusting in them
I will never stop,
I will simply keep walking
On and on,
Until all comes to an end

I will head ever forward,
As they push me onward

Excerpt from Yuya Tokisaka's lecture 'Ethics in Exorcism' held at the New York branch, 2037

Many have attempted to create homunculi Exorcists with ideal qualities to reduce casualties. Fraulein Faust was the first, but her homunculi were too weak and came at a heavy cost to create. A decade later, Fraulein Faust's student, M.V. Chell attempted to create a more refined battle homunculi. The result instead acted more like a child, seeking love and affection. M.V. Chell destroyed her research notes and disappeared. Over the next two centuries, the focus moved to enhancing Exorcists rather than creating them. This was primarily done through the testing of supposed enhancement serums, but none were successful. Then, in 2000, a researcher named Nao Yurasawa enhanced a child still in the womb with an influx of negative energy. The result was born in October that year, Yelena Heinman. As a child, she exhibited greater potential than any other Exorcist her age. As she grew, Yelena became exceptionally powerful. However, Yelena proved devoid of empathy, craving excitement above all else. She wiped out all the project researchers and her mother out of boredom. After this, the Exorcist Order outlawed all human experimentation by its members.

Chapter 7:
Vs Kyoko and Erica

Yelena ducked under Kyoko's blade.

'Blood Spears!' Yelena moved to strike with her right arm. Erica raised her fist. Yelena's blood spears did not appear. Erica's fist hurtled into Yelena's torso and made Yelena stumble backward. It was only then, that blood spears sprouted from her right arm.

Oh, I get it. Erica's technique allows her to slow the flow of negative energy, which slows my techniques to a crawl. How wonderful. It's a spectacular technique. That's how she was able to hit me when we first started fighting. I thought she would make this fight boring. I went through the trouble of hurting Yuya to get Kyoko to fight me without holding anything back—

Yelena ducked underneath another punch from Erica.

—but in calming Kyoko down, Erica has made this fight even more interesting. Last time, I heard about the vessel of Lucifer, Julie. Man, what a disappointment. Even after I smashed her into the ground, nothing happened. All that effort and Lucifer didn't even bother to show!

Kyoko lunged her blade at Yelena's temple. Yelena evaded with a dive. This left her vulnerable to Erica, who swiftly kicked her in the stomach with such force that she rolled across the ground.

Then, without regard for her life, Kyoko came at me with vicious fury. She inflicted this beautiful scar on my hand. Without any true power of her own, put me into a true battle for my life. It was the most fun I ever had. Who cares about Exorcists and demons? Kyoko is the most exciting to fight.

Yelena leapt back to her feet with a laugh.

'Thank you so much, Kyoko and Erica. This truly is the greatest. You can't know how grateful I am.'

I have to wait for an opportunity. Then I'll use Erica's own technique against her by hitting her with a surprise delayed attack. I can't attack until then. I have to wait.

'My life used to be so boring. It started in a stupid lab not too far from here. They ran tests on me and blabbed on and on about how I was an ultimate something-or-other.' Yelena still smiled as Erica pummelled her guts and Kyoko came within millimetres of slicing open an artery. Had Yelena not bent backward she would have received more than a small cut on her right brow.

Fun! Fun! Fun! It's exquisite!

'So eventually, I got bored and killed them all, even my stupid, crying mother. Geez, she was annoying.' Yelena rolled her eyes as Kyoko swung at her abdomen.

As Yelena ducked, Erica kicked the scratch Kyoko had made on Yelena's thigh. Blood burst out of the wound. The rush of pain made Yelena's smile broaden.

So intense! So wonderful! This is a real battle!

'But after that, I got bored again. Even after going into the outside world, even after joining Kujo, even though I could eat and kill at whim. I was empty. Nothing could fill me, no matter what I did. Then I fought against you, Kyoko, and that changed everything!

All this time, I've wanted to recapture that feeling.' Yelena licked the scar on her hand.

Yes. This is the fight I wanted. It's amazing!

'But now, it's even better than I could have imagined. This intensity, this animosity, the sheer violence... I have to thank you both, this is truly the best. I'm— I'm—'

My heart trembles! That's right, right now I'm—

'—having fun!' Yelena proclaimed as she outstretched her arms and looked up to the heavens. Erica took the opportunity to rush in, going right for Yelena's depraved head.

Now, time for the last act.

Yelena burrowed blood from her foot into the ground. She used a large amount of negative energy to separate and shape it. Erica's fist flung Yelena to the ground, delaying the technique. A few instants later, a blood-red anvil burst from the ground and slammed Erica to the pavement. Erica coughed up blood. Yelena jumped to her feet and immediately saw Kyoko come for her head.

This is the moment!

Yelena was forced to evade a sudden burst of lightning. She didn't bother to check where it came from. It was clear that it came from Jacob. Yelena knew he had exhausted the vast majority of his negative energy earlier. That attack had been the very last of his negative energy. Jacob had used those last drops of power to give Kyoko an extra few seconds. Within those few seconds, Kyoko got dangerously close. She entered the striking zone, leaving Yelena in a perilous situation if she did not properly defend.

Our finale!

'Kyoko! One last strike. Work with me,' Erica called out as she stumbled to her feet. She smirked as she clasped her hands together. Yelena swiftly sprouted blood spears across her upper torso and arms.

Even better, I'll use Erica's technique to my advantage. I'll leave my neck open whilst I simultaneously activate a delayed blood technique, leading Kyoko to be misled. Her blade will be deflected, then I'll bring the climax with a final blood attack.

Kyoko's blade cut Yelena down, slicing her in two across her stomach. Yelena's upper torso fell to the ground. Still alive upon the ground, she saw an exhausted Erica smirk.

'What? Haven't you heard of bluffing?'

'A bluff... But how did...'

'It was clear you had figured out Erica's technique, that you had prepared another delayed technique. When Erica called out, you clearly gestured toward your neck and left it so obviously open. You thought I would go for your neck, since I have been trying to take your head for so much of this battle. It was clearly your deception, so I went for the area you neglected,' Kyoko said coldly with a disgusted scowl.

'I see...' As Yelena spoke, she found herself both overjoyed and fearful.

So beautiful, but... I don't want to die. I can't fight anymore if I die.

The internal conflict fuelled her silence. The look on Kyoko's face burned with an intensity that rivalled Yelena's frozen joyful expression, an opposite force.

Her... hatred... It's so... frighteningly... beautiful... It's wonderful...

'You could never escape me. Your death was inevitable. You seek to kill without thought, to harm your fellow human beings with no consideration for anything except your own pleasures,' Kyoko said. 'I protect the people around me, help those precious to me and those who need it. At first, I hated you from a moral standpoint. I thought of you as a disgusting human being who enjoys hurting others. Now, I understand that my hatred comes from something far more simple and intense. That's why there was no other outcome than your death. That's why I had to kill you. In fact, even if you come back, even if you heal, even if you return to life or reincarnate, it won't change. Again, again and again. Over and over. I'll kill you. Not for morals or society, but because I hate you, I hate that all you do is destroy and hurt all that I love. That's why I'll hatefully kill you every time before you can hurt my world. Time and time again, I will kill you.' Kyoko's eyes burrowed into Yelena. Her words coursed through Yelena.

She's truly a devil! And yet... She's beautiful. A deity of death and despair. It's so immensely gorgeous. But I don't want to die. I want to kill and fight her over and over again. It's scary, scary, scary. It's not fair. I don't want to let this happen. But it's wondrous. It's amazing. Her cold hatred is the amusement I sought for so long. It's the best. I'm so scared. I'm so happy. This is the best way life could be, a true end to my boredom. What is this? To feel so much? Is this what they call love? Yes, Kyoko, I feel so much toward you. Perhaps I... Yes... She is the only person that I...

'I love you.' Yelena's fear, happiness, doubt, pleasure, thoughts all blended into a final wild smile as the life drained from Yelena. It was a smile devoid of all logic and reason. It sent a cold shiver down Kyoko's neck.

'You really killed her. I'm impressed, though I thought you would. Well done. How about you become my ally?' A voice behind Kyoko asked. She spun to find a tall man in a kamishimo stood behind her, a soft smile upon his face as though he was simply stepping in for a chat.

'Careful! That's Kujo!'

'I know, Erica. I'll end this right here.'

The End

Born into this broken world,
Only killing could satiate my soul
That is why, I am sad
For I can kill no longer
Such is my final despair
However,
Such is laced with hope
A brilliantly dark hope that cut me down
A hope named Kyoko Nakamura
My beloved hope,
Though I resent death taking away my pleasures,
I thank it for bringing my greatest one
For in body and soul,
I have been awed by your glory

Excerpt from *The Rejection of Gestalt: The Messiah's Journey* **by Yokoharu Satoimo, 2010**

The young man picked up his sword.
'For the sake of my friends, I will strike you down! You want me to feel pity for you?! You want me to understand you? I won't! I won't let you control this world anymore! I'm giving the power of this to the people! For my friends, I will strike you down and remake this world!'

The young man swung his weapon and struck down the last of the old gods.

Chapter 8: Vs Kujo

'Kyoko Nakamura, would you like to hear my reason? That which drives me to upend the world?' Kujo began. 'I guarantee it will be worth your—' he stopped as Kyoko rushed toward him.

'I suppose I will have to make you listen,' Kujo conceded with a sigh. He blinked.

Kyoko froze in place. Her eyes darted about while the rest of her body was completely still.

'Soul Photography: Restraint. Back in the Edo period, there was a superstition that cameras stole souls, trapping them forever within photographs. This technique stems from that superstition. By blinking and capturing an image of a person in the mind's eye, one can restrain the soul of that person. The soul of a person is merely the data of their body, hence, controlling the soul gives complete access to the body,' Kujo explained. He raised his right index finger and nodded.

Kyoko's eyes focused up to Kujo. Erica and Mikoto tensed. Jacob raised his fists.

'He's even stronger than we thought,' said Erica. 'He could have killed us three—no—five times over if he wanted by now. Let's just wait and listen to him, alright? Let's all calm down.'

Erica concealed her balled fists in her pockets.

Jacob sighed and lowered his hands. However, Kyoko knew the real target of Erica's words was her.

She's right. I lost sight of the plan. I need to calm down. Distracting Kujo right now is a good idea. It will give Caroline time to move in.

Kyoko closed her eyes. Her brow softened as she slowly exhaled. Kyoko opened her eyes. They were as still as water.

'Ah, good. You are ready to talk then.' Kujo blinked once more. Kyoko nearly fell forward as she regained control of her body all at once.

'So, tell me, just what the hell is your plan? Why do all this? Bring all this suffering?' Kyoko glared into Kujo's dark eyes.

Kujo smiled. 'To answer that question, allow me to ask my own. How are techniques gained?'

'We inherit them. Obviously,' Jacob interjected.

Kujo chuckled. 'Very good, but that's not the entirety of it. Think back to what I said before, that my technique is based upon the superstition of photography. Before that point, there was no such superstition. The original user of the technique was the first of his bloodline to ever use it. So then, how are techniques gained? The answer is rather simple. God grants us techniques.'

'What?' Erica exclaimed.

'But, how could that be true?' Mikoto asked.

'Impossible. All Exorcists know that the old gods are long dead.' Jacob said through a repressed stammer.

'The existence of God is entirely true, although the word "God" may be evoking the incorrect image. Allow me to use the term coined in Exorcist literature, the Administrator. It fits far better for the being that oversees this world. I used the English term "God" because he is a singular all-powerful being that governs this world, one that actually used to be an ordinary human two thousand years ago. In those times, this world was governed by the old gods of legend and myth. However, that man destroyed them all and usurped them because he sought a better world. The Administrator is the one who oversees this world and works to maintain order within it. Demons are creatures he has no control over, beings that cannot be eradicated nor completely sealed away. As long as human beings exist, so too will there be demons. Hence, the Administrator shapes the souls of humans to keep the demons in check. These humans are those we know as Exorcists. By touching our souls he grants us the use of negative energy to perceive demons and to manipulate techniques. A technique is either randomly inherited at birth from a direct blood relative who possessed said technique, actively selected to be inherited by the Administrator or forged entirely anew and bestowed to a select person. Although, that has not occurred for nearly half a century now. The Administrator's choice of technique is based upon whims and experiments. For example, four hundred years ago, he began to test if what truly mattered was human will or pure power. To that end, he gave Akihiko Nakamura immense physical potential and reflexes, in exchange for no technique and no negative energy.'

'Nakamura? Hold on, does that mean—'

'Yes, Jacob. He was the husband of the fifth Nakamura clan leader,' Mikoto said with a nod as her gaze drifted to Kyoko.

'What does that mean? Did I inherit my physical capabilities from him?' Kyoko said.

'Correct. The Administrator made it so the descendants of Akihiko would inherit this power as a recessive gene. You are the only one fortunate enough to have received it in all this time.'

'Fortunate.' Kyoko bit her lip.

I couldn't even stop Yelena from hurting my friends. How is that fortunate?

'I apologise. Please forgive my thoughtlessness. I am sure that to you this gift was not so bright. The Nakamura lost their way after all. Akihiko and Tomoko's legacy was ruined by their foolish descendants. Those brats who grew to only care for the power they were gifted from Tomoko's blood. Those fools who looked at you, their first-born child, and scorned you while being ignorant of your great power. Akihiko Nakamura was the strongest and most noble person I had ever met. You are quite like him. Your strength is a wellspring dedicated to the protection of others. In fact, your power is one that even the Administrator could fear in time, especially since you have my dear friend's blade, the only weapon humanity has possessed that could fell a god. And yet, you are a victim of this world. You were scorned by your family. You were forced into isolation. That is why I wish for you to join me, to make this world right, to help a victim like you.'

'A victim? But I decide my own life! I—'

'True, but then why has the Administrator allowed you to suffer? Is there truly a just reason for allowing children to suffer as he simply watches?'

'Hold on, but you put those demons in our path! And Yelena! What right do you have to make that claim?' Erica roared.

'I had faith you children would destroy those weaker beings. As for Samael and Lucifer, I am sorry. I needed Lucifer to appear, so I goaded Samael to pursue Julie, whilst keeping him ignorant of Lucifer. Yelena, on the other hand, was an offering. I found her running amok not long after you all encountered her and I thought this would save you some trouble in taking care of her. After all, scum must be destroyed quickly.'

'What the hell do you want?'

'It is simple. All of you—no—all the children of this world are victims. So, to save you all, I seek to change this world! The Administrator causes suffering and grief just to observe the results. He pits Exorcists in this unending battle and does nothing to make it easier. Not only that, but no matter the era, he has not done anything to help normal humans. The Administrator gave me two techniques. The first is the immortality technique. After the age of twenty-one, I ceased to age. For a thousand years, I have watched the same cycle of suffering over and over again. Naught has been done about it. That is why I must face the Administrator. I must destroy him and take his place!'

'Geez, you're always so gloomy. Guess it's up to me to stop you,' a voice suddenly called out in a playful sing-song. A woman with a majestic large afro wearing a jet-black biker jacket stood behind Kujo. The woman's presence had not been clear, none of her students had even been aware of her presence until she spoke. She stepped out from the shadow and into the moonlight. The moonlight illuminated her smirk.

'I should have known. Hello, Caroline. It's been about ten years, has it not?' Kujo said with a smile as he turned his head to face Caroline.

'Just about that, Master.'

'Are you truly trying to stop me? As yet another victim of his world, you know the Administrator is wrong, that he treats this world like a game.'

'Yeah, but that's not something you get to decide. Your methods are completely wrong. It's these children who have to change the world, down here amongst the humans. You want to open a portal to The Room of Creation, a portal that will tear apart the fabric of this world, that will destroy the land directly underneath it and destroy the entire world if it isn't closed in one day.'

'I will not let the world end. It will be a small sacrifice that will prelude the rebirth of the world I will restore the land and rid human beings of demons forever as the new Administrator. I will ensure no one suffers again, that this eternal cycle of suffering finally comes to an end.'

'But the people who die because of you can never be brought back to life, even with all that power. Besides, that new world would just be a lie, a facsimile of the precious world we all suffer and laugh in. I won't let you burden my students with so many deaths or to destroy their future, Kujo."

'It is unfortunate that you do not understand. I am truly sorry that you do not, Caroline.'

'Save it. We're here to fight.'

'But, I do not need to fight. My goal has already been achieved. You recall my second technique, do you not?'

'The Recreation Technique. It allows you to recreate any technique you directly touch.'

'Well, that was how it was ten years ago, but I can now recreate any technique my negative energy touches. Now, I can recreate all the techniques we have observed today.'

'What?!' Jacob said.

'Damn it!' Kyoko cursed.

'Damn you! Just what the hell are you doing, Kujo?' Erica gritted her teeth.

'I'll tell you, dear girl. I'm going to open the path to the Administrator's dimension! A realm normally unreachable will be opened. By combining Samael's

Time Distillation Technique, Lucifer's Spatial Destruction Technique, and Erica's Remote Energy Manipulation Technique, I have the key.' A dark nebula burst through the air. Kujo laughed as it appeared. Kyoko gripped her sword tightly.

I can't do anything. All I can do is watch while this bastard has his way. Damn it. Damn it!

'Hold Technique: Five Months,' Caroline calmly chanted. The portal reversed its flow, bent backward as the nebula of chaos and energy began to flow away. It fizzled until only a faint crack remained in the air. It sat against all laws of physics, simply resting in the sky.

'I see,' said Kujo. 'It appears as though you have also improved your technique over these last ten years. It works on phenomena as well as people now. You can actively pause even the most extreme from occurring. Five months is the maximum, is it not?'

'Well, I can manage seven, but five is all I need.'

'Oh?'

'See, by the time five months pass, these kids will surpass you. I'll train them beyond their limits. They will be able to change the world without destroying it. No, they absolutely will change the world with their own hands, gods and Administrators be damned!' Caroline grinned.

'How will they do that? How will they change this world? Do you have any idea how these children could do such a thing?'

'No clue in hell, but I have faith in them. I know they will change this world.'

'I see. No matter. In five months the result will still be the same. I simply have time to fill.' Kujo shrugged.

'Don't get cocky. I guarantee Kyoko here will kick your arse in five months.'

Master Caroline, can I really? I can't do anything

now! What makes you say that?! What gives you faith in us at all? None of us are even close to his strength.

'Is that so?' Kujo moved his gaze to Kyoko.

I... I...

'Yep! Come on, Kyoko, tell the bastard.' Caroline placed a hand on Kyoko's shoulder, with a smirk.

Yeah, I can do this.

'Right. I will defeat you!' Kyoko pointed her blade toward Kujo.

Kujo stared for a moment. He chuckled.

'Is that right? I look forward to that, Kyoko Nakamura. Until we meet again.' Kujo vanished into the breeze. The air cleared and silence reigned. The battle in Adelaide was over. The night was at an end, the light of the sun finally washing over the empty city.

Prologue

The pieces battle
Only seeing the truth now
Here ends our prologue

Final Chapter: Vs The Future

The rain fell on the empty city. Puddles of water pooled in the streets as thunder boomed in the air. Kujo sat cross-legged, his eyes closed until he heard footsteps softly clack against the wet stone. A blonde woman with porcelain skin and blue eyes walked toward him holding aloft a pink umbrella. Her frilly red dress with white sleeves and cuffs swayed with her steps.

'I had assumed the Paladins were busy dealing with Letrith's advance in Nigeria. Just what are you doing here?' Kujo eyed the woman.

She stopped directly in front of him, knelt and raised the umbrella above both of them as her blue eyes met his gaze.

'Yes, that is quite a good distraction,' the woman said. 'That should keep them busy, even for the next five months. To think you made a pact with an all-powerful demon king, merely as a distraction to keep the Order busy during your coup d'etat on the Administrator... Or rather, to keep Saki Sato busy. Her God Hands technique must be troublesome for you. She can alter its reality to ensure you can't copy it and she's the only Exorcist to ever defeat The Null Woman, June Dakota, in battle. You not only managed to keep the Order away, but your most troublesome enemy, yet you are so hopeless you do not even have an umbrella. Honestly, you are such a troublesome man, Toji,' The woman puffed.

'Toji, huh?'

'Please do not tell me you also have gone through an incredibly delayed rebellious phase and changed your name.'

'No, no. It is odd to hear my given name spoken again. It has been at least a decade or two since I have heard it.'

'That tends to happen when you make yourself an enemy of the world.'

'Perhaps that is why it feels so nice to hear it again, from you, my friend.'

'My, that certainly had an impact. I just wish it would make a responsible man of you,' the woman said through a deep exhale.

'And yet here you are, ignoring all that responsibility and, worst of all, your dear friend's question. You just follow your whims, as usual, and find yourself unbound by the rules that normal Exorcists face. You're quite the troublesome woman yourself, Faust,' Kujo chuckled.

'I am a selfish woman. There is no changing that. I suppose it is my nature. I still have not learned to put the world on my shoulders like you. Sorry, whims and bonds are all that drive me.' Fraulein Faust gave a small smirk as she placed a hand on her chin.

'That's not a bad thing. It's good you still have a connection to life. You know, when you made that sword with Sukeroku, I was worried you would use it on yourself to end this unending torment. Yet, thankfully you are still here.'

'To be honest, I did make it with the intention of ending myself, but I want to observe people just a bit longer. You are putting too much faith in me. I am just a cowardly and selfish woman.'

'What is so bad about that? Your selfishness is why you are still in this world, so it is surely a blessing.'

'My, what a speech.' Fraulein Faust chuckled.

'I suppose.' Kujo shrugged with a grin. Sunlight fell upon him as the clouds above separated.

'Just when I think I have seen everything, what marvellous timing.' Fraulein Faust slowly rose to her feet, shook the water off her umbrella and closed it up. Her was gaze fixed on the soft morning sky.

'Faust, are you here to join me?'

'Of course not.'

'Are you going to fight me?'

'Do not be silly.'

'I see. Then why are you here?'

'I had a whim to cover a dear friend from the rain and then see him off.' Faust smiled, eyes still set on the sky.

'Thank you, my friend.' Kujo stood and lowered his head into a small bow.

'You foolish man, there is no need to thank a woman like me for her whims. Well, my tasks are done. I will be off now.' Faust turned on her heel and began to walk away.

'Whims, huh? Was it on a whim that you gave Kyoko Nakamura the Black Blade? Or is there some plan of your design in motion?'

Fraulein Faust stopped and turned her head back to Kujo.

'An impulse for sure. She just reminded me of someone.' Faust smiled softly.

'Who?'

'A moron who sits in the rain.'

'Is that so?'

'It is. Well, I must be off. Farewell.' Faust waved as

she turned from Kujo. She walked into the distance.

'I see...' Kujo chuckled as he gazed up into the sky.

06/04/2035 1:00 PM

The small boy was in a field of mist, he fired his pistol over and over again. The mist slowly faded, corpses surrounded the boy; filled with bullet holes. He looked upon them, his hands shook while he bit his lip.

'You can't run away, this is your life. Let us continue wiping the filth from the world,' a man's voice echoed in the boy's ear.

'But I... I have friends now master, I don't need to kill anyone anymore. Why can't I be free?' The boy's voice echoed across the field of corpses. The man chuckled.

'Because you are always ours, you have killed people after all. Ever since you were sold to us, no, since you killed for us, that has been so.'

'No! I am free! I won't kill ever again!' The boy screamed as he threw the pistol on the ground. The pistol bounced and clacked until it landed near a pair of boots, the girl in the long ponytail picked the gun up.

'Kyoko? No! Stop!' The boy desperately ran towards her, Kyoko cocked the hammer and pulled the trigger into the mist. Blood splattered onto her from all directions. Tears rolled down her eyes as she gazed at the boy.

'No, Kyoko... I! I won't let you become a killer like me!' The boy screamed.

Ethan opened his eyes and was greeted by a calm white light upon a mellow ceiling.

'A hospital?' He whispered, his heartbeat slowed as he gradually took in his surroundings

'You're awake! Hey, everyone, Ethan's finally awake!' Veronica's voice came from Ethan's left.

He turned to see her seated on a chair. Her eyes were wide as a relieved smile reached her cheeks. Ethan felt a sharpness in his chest.

Damn, I didn't want anyone to trouble anyone. I was trying to help those guys. Wait! The battle! I was trying to ensure they didn't have to kill anyone. Yelena and Kujo too. I have to get moving.

Ethan thrusted himself upward, but was stopped by a wave of pain that surged through him.

'What are you doing? Stop. Calm down.' Veronica swiftly stood and placed her hands upon his shoulders.

'But the battle. I have to go and—'

'It was over two days ago, so calm down and listen, fool,' Atuy said as he entered the hospital room followed by Yuya, Jacob and Mikoto.

'Did you guys kill Yelena and Kujo?'

'Kujo got away, but Kyoko killed Yelena,' Mikoto answered.

'How did Kyoko look? Did she hesitate? Was she in pain?'

'Kyoko cut Yelena in half without hesitating. Yelena did hurt Yuya real bad after all. But then, she was kinda frightening, talking about her hate and how she would always kill Yelena,' Jacob said quietly.

So Kyoko was forced to become a killer. She embraced her hatred. Damn it. That was my burden. I've already killed. My soul is already dirty. She shouldn't have had to stain hers. It's my fault. I should have killed Yelena. But now... Because of my weakness... They've seen the world of killing...

'I wasn't able to do anything... I'm Sorry...' Ethan looked downward.

'No, you survived. That is enough,' said Mikoto warmly. 'We all survived. That is a clear victory. Besides, you spent so much negative energy that my healing was only able to provide basic first aid. That illustrates your effort. My technique heals best when negative energy circulates throughout the subject's body, acting as an enhancement to my innate healing power. Yuya's injuries were easy to heal because he had plenty of negative energy left. Veronica and Atuy took a little bit of time, since they only had a very small amount left in them. But you had used all of yours. That proves you put everything you had into this battle. It sure made healing you difficult though. I was only able to seal all your wounds and stop the bleeding. The proper healing will still take a few more days and be the doing of your own body.'

Ethan's irritation and doubt remained, but he found himself no longer entrenched within his emotions.

'Right. Thanks for healing me,' Ethan said.

'No problem whatsoever.' Mikoto gave a small smile.

'Yeah, you did good. I was only able to help for a bit,' Yuya said, his gaze on the floor.

'Don't put yourself down, man. You helped us. Honestly, it was a tough fight. Erica and Kyoko really clenched it by the skin of their teeth. The truth is our enemies are ridiculously strong. I mean, Yelena was super strong. It took everything we had to beat her. Then, Kujo... He... He's...' Jacob trailed off.

'That man is a true monster. Even if all of us had attempted to fight him all at once at our absolute best, he surely would have won with striking ease.' Mikoto bit her lip.

'You're right. We saw a monster too, one that I think none of us could ever beat,' Veronica said.

'Yes, she was truly a beast beyond what we could

possibly imagine. No one is at fault. Our enemies are just simply at a level of strength that is truly hard to comprehend,' Atuy said.

Everyone's eyes met the ground. The air became awkward.

'Why is everyone so silent?' Erica's voice broke the mood. She leaned against the doorframe with a cocky smile.

'It's just that—'

'What? You're all gloomy because our enemies are strong? Then just get stronger.'

The others gaped at her.

'We have five months until Kujo will come back, five months to become stronger. So, we're going to train together. Our bodies will scream. The world around us will become hell itself. Are you prepared, willing, to do this, my precious little brothers and sisters?' Erica outstretched a hand toward the others.

'Of course, elder sister,' Mikoto replied with a firm nod.

'Yeah. I'm going to jet this.' Jacob smirked.

'I'll do my best.' Yuya nodded.

'I will put my entire being into this endeavour.' Atuy flicked his glasses upward.

'I'll protect everyone, no matter what,' Veronica held her hands together.

'You're an idiot. Why are you so dramatic, Erica? But I get where you're coming from. I can't say I don't feel the same. Alright then, I'll go full force.' Ethan raised his fist. Determination burned through it.

This time, I will ensure that they don't need to see it again. This time, I won't let any of these guys kill. To protect them, I will kill Kujo myself.

'Glad to hear it,' Erica chuckled. 'Alright, let's aspire to new strength.'

'Wait, hold on. I just realised, where are Kyoko and

Julie?' Ethan asked. The others looked around the hospital room. There was no sign of them.

Erica smirked. 'Already training. Their process is just a little special is all.'

In the dark underground corridor, Kyoko and Julie stood before Caroline. The room stretched out almost without end, but somehow felt claustrophobic. The walls were packed with talismans, and the room was lit with a piercing yellow light.

'You two are special cases. Julie, you need to be able to control the power within you. Remember, Lucifer's power of space can destroy even the most powerful demons and gods. Kyoko, you can't control any negative energy at all, but you have Fraulein Faust's Black Blade. It's the only weapon that can kill Master—sorry—Kujo. To that end, I'm going to personally train you two. I will spar with the both of you day in and out, for months on end. In doing this, I'll push you two to the brink. Julie, this should allow you to become stronger in mind and body, and hone your battle sense. You should be able to become strong enough to use Lucifer's techniques. Kyoko, for you, this training won't unlock any new abilities, but it will develop your current ones, bringing your strength and reflexes to an entirely new level. You'll be a war god. However, I warn you two, this training will be hell. I can't guarantee the two of you will succeed. You can choose to leave now if you want. Once we begin, there is no turning back,' Caroline explained.

Kyoko and Julie slapped their hands together in a high five.

'I won't let Lucifer hurt anyone again. Please, train

me,' Julie said, her resolve steeled.

'I trained like crazy, but I was barely able to beat Yelena with help from my friends. I wasn't able to protect Yuya, and I wasn't able to do anything to stop Kujo. More than anything, I want to protect them this time. I want to save them. I never want to feel that powerlessness ever again. So please, teach me,' Kyoko said, her eyes set firmly on Caroline.

Caroline expected to see clouds of doubt or hesitation in her gaze. However, she only saw clear determination. Caroline chuckled.

Yeah, these unrelenting souls will be the ones to surpass and defeat you, Kujo. I know they will.

'Glad to hear it. Alright then. Welcome to hell!' Caroline smiled.

ADELAIDE GOURMET

Chapter 1: Tokyo and Hakata Ramen

A voice boomed like thunder throughout the small hall.

'Hey, Shin! We're back! Get us the good stuff!' The voice belonged to a tall woman with lacquered hair that stretched to her nape. Her dark eyes sparkled and her ruby lips assumed a wide toothy smile. Her creasy black business jacket, pants and crumpled tie swished wildly back and forth as the woman strode forward.

Shin looked up from his post at the counter of the small Japanese restaurant. The woman waved and skipped forward, her white sneakers squeaking as they met the marble ground. She would have continued to skip, had the short boy next to her not hissed through a glare.

'Moron,' snarled the short boy with long tied-back auburn hair, harsh ocean eyes and sharp thin lips. His business casual attire was spotless. He was silent as he softly stepped forward in his hushed brown loafers.

'Scary,' the woman said, before slowing into a regular walk with a sigh. Shin could not help but chuckle.

'Welcome, Colt, Maya. What can I get you this week?' Shin said with a warm smile.

'A Tokyo ramen, please,' Colt answered instantly.

'And a Hakata ramen for me,' Maya said as she put her arm around Colt's shoulder. Colt ducked under the arm and sat down at a table that had just been cleaned. Maya shrugged and joined Colt, who scowled.

'Coming right up,' Shin declared.

The restaurant was small, a charmingly humble clean little establishment with only five tables. Upon the walls were pieces of traditional Japanese art. Colt was fixated on the one known as *The Great Wave off Kanagawa*. Maya crossed her right leg over her left, bobbing the foot that was hovering in the air as she hummed a tune so bastardised it was impossible to know what song it was supposed to be. They continued quietly like this, until Shin came over with their food.

In front of them he laid two bowls filled with tender noodles, juicy Char-Siu, warm hardboiled eggs and nori swimming in warm soup. The difference in their ramen came from the fermented bamboo and fishcake swimming in the soft soy-pork broth of Colt's Tokyo ramen, in contrast to the diced ginger and shitake mushroom that floated upon the thick gravy-like tonkotsu broth of the Hakata ramen. Colt delicately took the soup spoon and took a satisfying slurp of the soft, but strong broth. He funnelled noodles into his mouth with the chopsticks. Maya ravenously slurped up noodles, gulped down a perfectly done egg in one mouthful, then thrusted Char-Siu into her mouth.

'Slow down,' Colt said with a sigh.

'But it's so good! Way better than Tokyo ramen. This flavour is bolder and stronger,' Maya retorted, pointing her chopsticks at Colt.

'Taste is a completely subjective interpretation of this world. It has no basis in objective factors. Only complete morons would try to use it to persuade another of wrongness,' Colt said as he ate a crunchy, but delectably juicy bamboo shoot.

'I shouldn't have expected anything else from you.

You're logical and to the point. Well, except for how you pick your food.'

'What do you mean?' Colt cocked his head.

Maya smirked. 'Well, you don't pick your food logically, do you? I mean, the first time you chose it you used logic to make a deduction, but that deduction wasn't about whether it would be healthy or not. Instead, what were you deducing? That ramen isn't any healthier or objectively better than mine, right? So why do you continue to order it every week?'

'Ah, I see. I deduced it would be popular, hence I chose it because it logically would be quite tasty. I continue to order it because I indeed found it tasty.'

'Ding, ding, ding! Correct answer.'

'Yes, I suppose my eating habits contradict the rest of my philosophy... But then many aspects of living are illogical, merely abject things that serve no true purpose, and yet people cling to these parts of life. I am no different. I am just another person, trapped in the illogical flow of life. The only difference being that I can see it because of my time outside,' Colt said.

Maya was silent, then laughed. 'That's such a "you" answer. So thoughtful, logical, angsty. But then, it seems you're enjoying yourself. Maybe I'm rubbing off on you?' Maya grinned.

'Piss off, tar lungs,' Colt said, turning away from Maya and focusing on his ramen.

'I thought you'd like my smoking, since it brings me closer to your oh-so-precious death.'

Colt slurped up the rest of his ramen broth. 'What I value is death itself. The method in which it actually occurs is irrelevant to me. I don't care if you smoke or what it does to your body, but it is irritating having to put up with the foul stench,' Colt said.

Maya went to open her mouth, but her phone buzzed. She pulled up the screen. Her eyes widened.

'They've appeared. Just a few blocks away.' Maya shovelled the rest of her food into her mouth. She released a satisfied exhale.

Colt had already finished. He stood and began to leave.

'Thank you.' He nodded to Shin as he left.

'Thanks again.' Maya sprung to her feet and bolted to Colt.

'Take care. Until next week.' Shin could not help but smirk at the two. Colt had come here every Monday for two years. Maya had started the tradition seven years ago. Shin recalled when Maya first brought Colt there. Even back then. there was no doubt the two of them were incredibly odd, even more so as a pair. However, Shin could not make such a judgement so easily. He himself was rather odd. With that thought, he chuckled as he watched Colt and Maya haste away.

The two little blonde girls' path down the street was blocked by Colt and Maya. Colt's eyes were cold and focused. Maya stepped forward with a grin.

'So you two are the notorious Dark Punishers, right? The homunculi that only kill criminals? Thank you for your service to society, but now it's your turn to die,' Maya whistled. She drew two serrated knives. Colt followed suit by brandishing a short sword.

'Just what are human beings? Nothing but lumps of ego and sin. Do not think that—'

Before the girl could finish her sentence Colt swiftly and cleanly removed her head from her shoulders. Blood burst from her exposed neck as her lifeless body tumbled to the pavement.

'Your judgements have no value without death.

They are merely perceptions of the world guided by chemical reactions. But after death they have value, the value held by those who understand those judgments and the inheritors who hold them as ties to those who have left this life. These connections and values give meaning to the lives people live. Without death, life cannot have value. Hence, I have returned you to humanity through death,' Colt proclaimed as he flicked the blood off his blade.

Before the other sister could react, Maya slit her throat open. Blood sputtered from it as the girl gasped for air. Her arms grasped at her neck in vain.

'Sorry, but even you homunculi can't regenerate from these bad boys,' Maya said, she grinned as she raised both her knives up beside her cheeks. 'You'll die in just a bit. I'm not going to give some philosophical lecture on what meaning your death has, or some bull like that. I don't really care. It's my job to kill you, so I killed you. To keep living this life, to keep being accepted, I kill and... Oh, you're already dead? Ah, well... Sorry for talking your ear off. I should have just let you die in peace.' Maya chuckled as she rubbed the back of her neck. Colt rolled his eyes and walked away. Maya chased after him.

'Were you really trying to leave without me?'

'Of course.'

'How mean.'

'Shut up.'

'Hey, hey! How about we get some dessert? Some cheesecake is always great after we finish an assignment!'

'I have no objections.' The two walked in search of delicate cheesy sweets, leaving two small corpses to rot in the uncaring city.

Next Chapter Preview:

The Three Memories

Disappointment

Would you forgive me?
I know that I have no worth
But please forgive me
Try Again
Please do not hate me
I will always keep trying
Until you accept me
Dance
I will dance for you
Around and around I go
Struggling for you

Chapter 2: Banh Mi and Cold Rolls

Maya lit the cigarette between her lips and sucked the smoke into her mouth. With it, came a flood of memories of the life she once shared with her parents and her days of failure at school. She always came home to disappointment. Worthless commands came from people shut off from the diversity of the world. Maya screwed her eyes shut and removed the cigarette from her mouth, trying to bury the memories of her wasted youth, it was futile. Fruitless attempts to fit in bubbled in her mind. Maya exhaled and the memories burst forth from her with smoke. She had always struggled and fell far behind the other children but Maya's parents did not provide her comfort. Instead, all they gave her were commands and ultimatums.

'You can do it, Maya. You just need to try harder.' Her father smiled.

Shut up.

'That's right. You can do it if you put in more effort. You just need to spend less time playing. Yes, let's make it four hours of studying every night.' Her mother nodded.

Shut up.

'Hmm... No improvement, huh? That's a shame. I suppose you haven't been working hard enough,' her father groaned.

Shut up.

'That's right! You just need to try harder, Maya. Let's go for five hours a night from now on.' Her mother clapped her hands.

Shut up!

'Yes, just keep going like this and you will surely improve,' her father agreed.

Shut up! Shut up!

'Absolutely! You'll be a good girl and work hard for Mummy and Daddy, right?' her mother said as she knelt to Maya's eye level.

Shut up! Shut up! Shut up! Shut up! Shut up!

'You're a good girl, right? Come on, Maya. Give Mummy and Daddy a big smile, alright?' Her father said, pointing his lips up into a smile with his fingers.

SHUT UP! I—I just—

'Here.' Colt shattered Maya's world of memories as he handed her an unfamiliar stuffed bread roll and started walking away.

'Oh, thanks,' the dazed Maya managed to stammer. She was grateful to be freed from the hell inside her. Maya pressed her cigarette into the ground, walked past a bin and tossed it in as she strode up to Colt's side, trying not to think about those worthless scum Maya had once known as her parents.

After all, my precious little co-worker is here.

As she walked beside Colt, Maya moved her focus to the bread roll and took a generous bite. She found a delicious mix of crispy bread, juicy barbeque pork, diced carrot, coriander, chilli and pâté.

'Whoa! This really works. The flavours all blend together perfectly to create a juicy, spicy, crispy bread roll!'

'Banh Mi. It comes from Vietnam. A combination of French-style bread, Chinese-style meat and local Vietnamese ingredients, creating a balanced and unique flavour,' Colt said sagely.

Maya stuffed the remainder of the bread roll into her mouth. Colt sighed and lifted a plastic container holding three translucent spring rolls.

'Here.' Colt gestured for Maya to take them. She picked one up and lifted it so it was level with her eyes.

'What are these?'

'Cold rolls. A special Vietnamese-style roll. Rice noodles, prawns—or sometimes pork—and vegetables are wrapped in rice paper to create a soft, but unmistakable, flavour,' Colt answered, taking a moment to finish off his Banh Mi. When Colt turned back to Maya, she had consumed all three cold rolls. Colt stared at her.

'Oh, sorry. They were just so good.' Maya's eyes darted in all directions.

'No, a Banh Mi is enough for me. It is just... I still cannot believe you have not choked to death yet.'

'Mean!'

'No, it is truly a miracle you have not choked at the rate you eat.'

'You're impressed?'

'Impressed and surprised are two vastly different things. It would be more accurate to say that I am...'

'Concerned? Worried? Fretful?'

'Baffled... Or... Hmm...' Colt turned his head to the water fountain they were walking past. In front of the fountain stood a meek black-haired teenage boy. The boy took deep breaths, his lip quivering and knees wobbling. However, Colt's eyes were focused on the fountain water, the clear water that did not reflect the boy.

Colt turned back and swung his sword at the boy's head. The boy leapt into the air, and Colt's swing cut one of the boy's legs off from the knee down. The boy hit the ground with a sharp scream. Blood slowly poured from his neatly cut leg.

'He had no reflection. We have to eliminate him,' Colt stated as he moved forward.

The boy used the inhuman strength in one of his arms to launch himself at Colt, but he landed far beyond Colt's reach. Maya followed the boy closely. Her blades swiftly struck a barrage of blows. Blood squirted from the cuts across the boy's torso.

'Damn you! Filthy hunter!' The boy spat between sharp breaths.

'Hey, don't say mean things like that. My job is to kill homunculi, regardless of the circumstances. That's how the higher-ups protect the peace. I'm just doing my job, give me some slack,' Maya said.

'How dare you be so flippant, you damn human!'

'See, I like my everyday life. My old life was a truer hell than the one I'm about to send you to. This world I live in now can only be called a paradise, a world where I can be me, where I am accepted, where I can do what I'm good at, where I have people who actually care about me. I only need to do one thing to keep this world, keep killing those who stand my way.' Maya's stare cut into the boy's quivering eyes, tears forming at their edges and falling onto pale cheeks.

'You're a monster!'

'Nah, I'm just a working woman.' Maya plunged her blade into the boy's temple. She wiped her brow and pulled the blade out.

'Good job,' Colt said as he sheathed his sword. Maya thrust her arm around Colt's shoulder.

'Praising me, huh? What a good boy. How about I treat you to something nice?' Maya cooed.

'Some ice cream would be nice,' Colt said plainly.

Geez, I was trying to mess with him. I can't help

but be fond of his cluelessness.

'Alright then, let's go.' Maya chuckled as she led Colt onward, to enjoy the spoils of her ordinary life.

Next Chapter Preview:

Worth

What value does courage have without fear?
Peace without war?
Food without hunger?
All these require each other to truly be valuable
So answer me this,
How can lives without death hold any meaning?

Chapter 3: Beef Fried Rice and Mapo Tofu

Colt placed the tray on the table and sat down. He studied the mound of fried rice stacked on an oval plate, topped generously with large chunks of beef, Chinese-style scrambled egg, thin slices of carrot and peas. Next to the plate was a bowl of Chinese soup. Colt grasped the spoon he had been given, dug a scoop of everything and placed it into his mouth. The mouthful contained a harmony of flavours. Juicy beef, salty egg, crunchy carrot and soft peas melted into the absorbent rice. A wondrous array of humble, yet distinct flavours.

'It's good,' Colt remarked. He placed more and more spoonfuls into his mouth.

'Uh huh, this place is so good,' Maya said, taking another mouthful of her Mapo Tofu, a dish in a distinct flat circular bowl with high edges. Inside lay a red chilli sauce, minced pork and thick cubes of tofu. Colt had never tried the dish, thus he could not attest to its taste. However, Maya's positive reaction seemed to be a good indicator that it was delicious.

To think this is all chance...

They had been passing through Chinatown, going through the food court on the way to a job. In the process Maya happened to notice a stall that sold simple Chinese cooking. It stood out from the other brighter restaurants, appearing plain and humble. Maya expressed interest and Colt relented, but they ordered regardless.

Interesting...

Before his thoughts could truly drift off, Maya loudly coughed and sputtered.

'So hot!' She grasped her throat. Colt sighed.

'Idiot, did you think a dish with so much chilli sauce would be mild? You drank all your soup too early as well. Go buy a drink from there.' Colt pointed to the stall at the far end of the court, the one advertising beverages from all across the world.

Maya swiftly stood, waved goodbye and bolted to the stall. Colt ignored her as he finished the last few bites of his fried rice, downing them with his refreshing soup. Colt didn't have long to sit in satisfaction. He noticed a young woman with dark hair walk through the food court.

The target!

He got to his feet and followed her calmly. Colt's steps were small and quiet. His hand sat in his pockets and his face was vacant. Only from the corner of his eye, did Colt focus on the woman. The woman turned into an empty alleyway.

Damn! She must have noticed me. I have to take her out now.

Colt walked into the alleyway. The young woman with dark hair turned to face him and smiled.

'So, kids like you can be hunters? What has this world come to?' She shook her head, eyes tightly shut. Colt drew his sword and stepped forward, poised to strike down the woman.

'No hesitation, huh? I thought a kid would be bothered by killing. That's truly sad. Killing shouldn't be undertaken so easily, especially not by children.'

'Only by killing you, can I make you human.'

'So you think that killing is the right thing to do? Killing is never the right thing to do. We all have dreams, thoughts, feelings. Killing just wastes those.' The woman stared at Colt intently.

Those eyes... Is she pleading? No, she is a homunculi. It is merely an act. Even if she is, it does not matter.

'You are wrong. Death is what gives life meaning,' Colt said coldly.

'What did you say?' the woman said, baffled.

'The value of life is defined by death. The fact that life is limited is what makes it special and gives it value. The fact we only have finite time to conduct our lives is what makes our experiences so precious and worth going through in the first place. To have infinite time, to be able to experience everything, to unendingly shape our perspectives and convictions. That would render life meaningless,' Colt said, steadfast in his conviction.

The woman paused. She winced as her hands tightened into fists.

Colt took this opportunity to attack. He swung for a decapitation. As his blade soared through the woman's neck with a plume of blood, he made eye contact once more. Colt lowered his head as he sheathed the blade.

'Now that it has ended, your life has value. I won't forget the beauty of your death,' Colt whispered, his hand trembled as he spoke. Colt shook his head and walked away.

Maya tapped the table impatiently. She had just gone to get a drink, but came back to find she was alone.

She downed the sweet Mexican cola she had purchased.

'I leave for a minute and he pisses off. Dammit!' Maya cursed. She wanted to light a cigarette, but the last time she tried to smoke in this food court the security guard had scolded her harshly.

'Even if you are irritated, do not smoke,' a familiar voice said. Colt sat down in the chair opposite of her.

'What the hell? You go off without a word and then go come back only to tell me off? Geez,' Maya muttered with a sigh. Colt clicked his tongue in irritation.

'So, where did you go?'

'I saw our target, so I followed her and took her out,' Colt said. Maya sprung up.

'What? You shouldn't have gone alone. This is why you need a phone,' she chided.

'I do not want one of those horrible boxes.' Colt shook his head.

'But if you had one you could have just texted or called me. It's not a matter of enjoyment. It's about convenience and safety. I mean, that was supposed to be a strong target. It's a good thing you're not a corpse.'

'I understand, but I do not want distractions. I wish to focus on enjoying my life,' Colt said with a soft smile.

Maya was struck into silence. Finally, she chuckled and sat back down.

'Alright, alright, you win. I can't argue there. Life is there to be enjoyed after all. Just make sure you stop doing stupid stuff like this, alright?' Maya said softly.

Colt nodded. 'I promise, but I do not want to end up like you. You enjoy life far too much. If I am not careful I might pick up some of your vices,' Colt chuckled.

Does he have any respect for—wait—was that a joke? Did he seriously just make a joke and not a judgement? Huh, I guess the little guy has grown quite a bit.

Maya smiled warmly.

Next Chapter Preview:

Ties

Big brother keeps fighting on
To preserve the ties he held, now lost forever
The young woman keeps on keeping on
To protect the ties of her life
The boy keeps walking
To see beautiful death

Chapter 4: Yum Cha

Years ago, Maya ran from the clutches of those de-
testable people who called themselves her parents.
She ran and ran until her legs were unable to carry
her. Maya did not know where she was. She did not
know what she was going to do next. Exhausted and
lost, she sat in the dirty street. Maya had wondered
if it had even been worth it, if she should just die and
stop feeling pain altogether. It was then that an odd
woman with nape-length red hair, an eyepatch over
her left eye and a cigarette in her mouth knelt in front
of Maya. The woman studied Maya, and exhaled a
puff of smoke right into her face. A weak cough came
from Maya's tired lungs. The woman's eyes widened.

'Whoa, you look terrible! I assumed you were a
corpse, but it appears you're still alive. I'm impressed.
You must be a pretty tough kid. So, are you a runaway? Actually, don't answer that. I know a runaway
when I see one. In fact, I bet you're a runaway because
you have nowhere to belong, since even at home no
one gave you recognition.' The woman smiled.

'So what?' Maya answered weakly.

'Well then, how about I give you a choice?' The
woman's eye sparkled.

'What choice?' Maya asked, her voice firmer as her
eyes narrowed on the woman. The woman's smile
deepened.

'I'll give you two choices. The first is I can leave

you here to die.'

'And the other?'

'I can give you an ordinary life, one where I won't force you to be something you're not, where I won't say "you're wrong." I won't tell you to hide your emotions or smile for me or to work harder. It'll be an unexceptional life, where you can eat when you're hungry, drink when you're thirsty, cry when you're sad, smile when you're happy and sleep when you're tired. Who knows, you might even find people who accept you. However, to have this life, you'll have to fight. You'll need to fight to protect this life and keep living it. You might even have to die for this life. So... What will it be?' The woman took the cigarette from her mouth as she gazed at Maya.

Maya and Colt each brought a tray. Maya's tray held several steamers full of dumplings ranging from meat Siu-Mai to sweet pork Char-Siu Bao, pork and chives Fun Guo, prawn Har Gow and a plate piled with fried squid. Colt's tray held a large teapot filled with Jasmine tea and a couple of white ceramic teacups painted with a dark blue dragon curled at the button of each cup.

They sat down. Colt poured the tea while Maya placed a bowl and a pair of chopsticks in front of each of them. Yum Cha was a rare treat. They mostly had it for celebrations or sometimes when their profession allowed time for a leisurely lunch. However, the rarity of their indulgence in Yum Cha also stemmed from Maya's first memories of the cuisine.

Four years prior, Maya's third work partner, Li Jie, had been offered a promotion. He accepted it without a second thought and to celebrate, he treated Maya to Yum Cha. He taught her about what dishes she should order in what quantities and how many people she should bring. After which, they sat down and ate ravenously. The words Li Jie told her between sips of tea were etched into her mind.

'Listen here, Maya. What I'm about to tell doesn't come from any traditions or culture. But I need you to listen to your senior one last time. Yum Cha is all about relaxing and enjoying yourself. You don't rush it. You don't prolong it either. You merely enjoy it. That's why you can't have it every day. You can only have it when you have time to relax, alright? But that's not all. You have one more condition to meet before you can have Yum Cha. This is the kind of food that's boring to have alone, so always have another person to eat it with. It can't be just anyone either. It must be someone you truly like, since eating with someone you hate is worse than dying a thousand times. This might baffle you right now, you're only fifteen after all, but one day this will all be absolutely clear.'

Maya smirked. At the time she had just nodded but now she understood.

'What is this about?'

'Nothing really.'

'But generally, Yum Cha costs quite a bit. What is the occasion this time?' Colt persisted.

'Does it have to be about something? Why does it have to have a meaning beyond fulfilling an impulse? Always focusing on a purpose makes life so mechanical and boring. People make up labels to give life more meaning than there is, but it's incredibly simple. If you're hungry, eat. If you're thirsty, drink. If you're sad, cry. If you're happy, smile. If you're tired, sleep. When the hell did we forget those simple truths? Just enjoy life, don't worry yourself with things that don't really matter, alright?' Maya raised her teacup to Colt, the soft gold liquid within her cup wavering.

'I understand. I suppose no reason is needed. Let us simply enjoy this meal then.' Colt raised his teacup and clinked it against Maya's.

'Yeah, let's enjoy it together,' Maya chuckled.

Conditions met, Li Jie, you annoying old geezer.

As Maya drank she noticed a tall man with long blonde hair. His sky-blue eyes stood out as they peered into her. However, in her tea, there was no reflection of the man.

Maya leapt into the air. Colt raised his blade into a defensive stance. In less than an instant later, the man slammed his arm into the table. The blow fractured the table in two and smashed the teapot into a hailstorm of ceramic white shards, while the liquid splattered across the ground. The food was scattered everywhere, a pulp of unrecognisable mess. Colt was knocked backward. His sword hummed from the blow it had just withstood. Maya landed in a crouch. Her heart pounded fast. Her breath sharpened.

The food... The tea... It's gone... Colt was... almost killed! My ordinary life is under attack!

In the depths of her mind, Maya recalled what she had been told the day she became herself.

'However, to have this life, you'll have to fight. You'll need to fight to protect this life and keep living it. You might even have to die for this life.' *My precious ordinary life is under attack. I have to protect it. I have to fight for it. Fight! Fight! Fight!*

The other patrons of the food hall scattered in all directions. Their bodies formed waves that crashed away from the battle. The man ignored them. His gaze was only focused on Maya and Colt. Maya stepped forward and drew her knives.

'I'll kill you!' Maya declared. She unleashed a flurry of attacks that the man barely avoided, caught off guard. The man thrust his hand toward Maya's neck. Colt's blade moved to intercept the hand, forcing the man to take a step back.

'Fool! What value would this death have to your ordinary life? Calm down! We will kill him together. When you die it must be meaningful. Do not die yet,' Colt commanded.

Maya took a deep breath. 'Sorry, I kinda lost my head, but this bastard has made it personal. I am going to kill him for ruining this,' Maya said, the waves in her mind returned to still waters.

'Good, you are back to simply being a fool.' Colt turned back to the man, a smile softly flickering on his lips. Maya smirked and followed his eyes.

The man stood frozen, eyes burning into Colt and Maya.

'Do you two recall killing my sisters? The twins? I am going to kill you both regardless of what you say, but tell me, why did you kill them?' The man said, each word laced with hatred.

'Life has no value without death. I gave their death-less bodies the chance to be human again. I will do the same for you. I will grant you death so your love for them will have value,' Colt resolutely answered, preparing to strike at any second.

'It was just business. It's my job to kill homunculi so I kill homunculi. Nothing else to it really. But you're a different story. By attacking my quiet life you made it personal. I'm going to kill you as payback,' Maya snarled.

'Filthy, arrogant humans,' the man cursed. He launched into an enraged assault.

Maya and Colt's blades bounced off his palms. Colt saw his opportunity and sliced off one of the man's arms. This gave Maya an opening to slit the man's throat.

Tears formed in his eyes. He looked upward and tried to speak but all that came out of his mouth was a gargle of blood. Wordless, the man's corpse hit the ground. His dead eyes glazed upward.

'I will not forget your feelings. Through death they have been immortalised,' Colt whispered as he sheathed his blade.

'That's what you get, arsehole! I'll fight to the death to protect this ordinary life and kill anyone who tries to destroy it! I hope you remember that in your next life, so you don't mess with my meals or my friends again. If you do, I'll kill you even worse next time!' Maya roared.

Next Chapter Preview:

The Two

Recollection
I still recall it
The day when I met that boy
A cool Autumn day
Another
He was the fourth one
Now the fifth one she brought here
Another killer
Unique
He was different
His eyes were so clear and blue
Full of gentle thoughts
A Pair
The odd happy girl
The quiet thoughtful boy
I recall them well

Chapter 5: First Tokyo and Hakata Ramen

Shin scrubbed a table as he whistled an old tune, enjoying the quiet before the restaurant opened. It was not that Shin did not enjoy people and noise, it was more that he enjoyed peace and quiet in equal measure. As such, he found serenity in wordlessly cleaning every morning.

Though this morning was slightly peculiar. He found himself thinking about Maya and Colt. Perhaps it was because Colt was his only regular interested in discussing philosophy, or perhaps it was because he had watched Maya grow up. Or perhaps it was neither. Perhaps they were in his head for no particular reason whatsoever. Regardless, Shin recalled the day two years ago when he had first met Colt, the day Colt and Maya became partners. Maya had given him an entire account once when they smoked together one time near the botanical garden. Maya's words drifted back to him, as though her cigarette smoke still hung in the air around him.

Maya's eyes were upon the rows upon rows of graves surrounding her. Trimmed grass blew in the quiet morning.

'Maya, I have your new partner,' a voice called behind her.

Maya turned her head back toward the voice. The woman with the eye patch smiled and exhaled from her cigarette, dropping ash upon the grass with a sizzle.

Beside the woman stood a short boy with long auburn hair. He wore a neat suit. Upon first inspection, Maya thought he looked far too delicate for this type of work. In Maya's experience, that kind of person either ended up quitting or died after one week. However, before she could protest, Maya noticed the boy's eyes. She could not articulate nor understand quite what it was, but she saw something intense and unmovable in his eyes. It piqued her interest.

Maybe he will be good for this work. Grace selected him, so he's probably got some talent. Alright then, I'll see what he's got.

'What's your name?' she asked.

'Colt,' the boy quietly answered.

'How old are you, Colt?'

'Fifteen.'

'I'm seventeen. That makes me your senior in both age and experience. You're my fifth partner. Grace here was my first before she got promoted. My second partner is in a grave four rows back. My third partner also got promoted and number four is in this charming grave right here. As you can see, in this job you either die or live long enough to move up in the world. I recommend listening to me, if you want to move up in the world.'

'I intend to do this for a long time. As long as it is not an act of foolishness, I will follow you,' Colt said without hesitation.

Maya smiled. 'I like you. Quiet, but with a mind of your own. I'll take him, Grace,' Maya chuckled.

'Is that so? Well, next week—'

'No, I'm going to put him to the test now. I wanna see what he's got.' Maya smirked.

'It's good to see you invested. Alright then, have it your way,' Grace said with a grin.

'Great! Colt, let's get going,' Maya commanded.

'Where?'

'Somewhere important,' Maya said as she walked off, forcing Colt to follow her.

'Are there targets here? Or perhaps an exchange of information?' Colt inquired.

Maya stopped before a small Japanese restaurant. 'Nope, we're having lunch.'

'Lunch?'

'It's important to have a good lunch in our profession. After all, we have to have enough energy to fight long and gruelling battles. Or what, did you seriously think cold-hearted killers didn't need to eat?'

'Alright then,' Colt conceded with a sigh.

'Good, you understand. This place is the best and super affordable,' Maya explained as she led him into the restaurant. Inside, Shin gave them a smile.

'Welcome! Hello again, Maya. And who is this? Your new partner?'

'Yeah, this cutie is Colt. It's his first day on the job. I'm giving him the proper breaking in, starting with some great ramen.' Maya smirked.

'I see. Well, don't be too hard on the poor boy.'

'Sure, sure, I won't. Anyway, I'll have the usual Hakata ramen.'

'Coming right up, and what would you like, Colt? Take your time. I can explain dishes if you don't know them,' Shin offered.

'No, no! Colt, you have to pick the ramen you think suits you best, without knowing what it is,' Maya declared.

Shin was about to protest when Colt pointed to the menu.

'Then I will have the Tokyo ramen,' Colt said swiftly.

'Coming right up.'

'Whoa! Good choice there! Now tell me, what made you choose it?' Maya asked, forcing her voice low and stroking her chin.

'Tokyo is a highly populated capital city, so I ventured that a dish named after it would be a popular dish and thus be pretty good,' Colt explained as though it were a matter of fact.

'Seriously? Way to kill the fun,' Maya sighed.

They sat down and waited in silence until Shin brought out their ramen. Maya immediately tucked into it, while Colt sampled it with a small mouthful of noodles.

'It is amazing,' he whispered.

'Do you see why I go here so often?'

'Yes.'

'Glad ya do, because it's practically a ritual. Once a week, every Monday, we come here.'

'I have no objection,' Colt said before going back to eating.

The two ate in silence until they finished. Shin went to take the bowls away when Colt noticed a small book in Shin's pocket. It was titled *The Mind on Fire*.

'I have long since learned, as a measure of elementary hygiene, to be on guard when anyone quotes Pascal,' Colt said without warning. Shin's eyes widened.

'So you're familiar with Pascal and Ortega?'

'Yes, I read their works and a few other philosophers.'

'If you don't mind, who else do you read?'

'Fukuzawa, Plato, Socrates, Kung Fu Tzu, Hegel, Krishnamurti.'

'Amazing! Most people your age, in fact, most people generally, don't have any interest in philosophers at all.'

'Well, I wanted to learn and think more about the world, and the meaning of life itself.'

'Hm... So then, what do you think is the meaning of life?' Shin beamed.

Colt paused and considered his answer. 'Death is what gives life meaning, for the limitation of death gives value and purpose to our lives,' Colt answered. Shin nodded, intrigued.

'Why are you being all philosophical? Trying to impress my new partner, Shin? Anyway, life is about belonging. People lie and kill so they can belong,' Maya said with a smirk.

'Hm...' Shin pretended to consider her point out of politeness, a politeness Colt did not share, completely ignoring Maya and turning to Shin.

'How about you? Do you have your own perception on the meaning of life?' Colt asked.

Shin's answer came without hesitation. 'My belief is rather simple: the meaning of life is infinite, for life can have any value or purpose we want. Its value is perceived and made different by every single living thing,' Shin explained grandly. He had never before had the opportunity to express his point of view.

'That's fascinating. I look forward to coming again.' Colt nodded.

'We sure will. I'm glad you get it, but let's do less philosophy next time, please? I like my brain not to melt before work,' Maya said.

'Fair enough, perhaps just a little philosophy then.

I look forward to seeing you both again then.' Shin smiled.

'What is that?' Colt asked suddenly.

Maya turned to see him pointing at the black rectangular box that neatly sat in the palm of her hand.

'You mean my phone?'

'That is a telephone?'

'Seriously? Didn't your parents have one of these? Or wouldn't you have learned about the modern world in school?'

'I do not have parents and I did not go to school.'

'Then what the hell kind of upbringing did you have? How do you not know these things?'

'I was raised on the outskirts of the hills. There was not much technology except for electric lights and running water. The old man who raised me taught me a lot of things. How to survive, how to cook, how to read and write using his old books. Although, the one thing he had no interest in teaching about was the world. He always said that was something I would have to learn for myself one day.'

'That actually explains a lot. Who was the old man to you? Your grandpa? An uncle? A family friend?'

'I do not know. I do not even know his name, even after his death. He told me he found me and decided to raise me on a whim. That is all I know about my past and his relation to me.'

'Then how do you know your name? Wouldn't he have known your parents? Or if he named you, wouldn't he have told you his name?'

'Actually, the old man just used to address me as "you" or "child" and I just called him "you." However, when I was eight, I read Soseki Natsume's Botchan. The story placed great value on names and labels, which led me to become deeply interested in them. I asked the old man what my name was. His colt revolver was on the table behind me, so he gave me the name Colt and said I could just call him "old man",' Colt said.

'I see... Thanks for answering,' Maya finally said, her brow knotted.

'It is no issue.'

'Ha, you're so dry and yet so interesting. I like you even more than I thought I would. I sure hope you can do this job well and be my partner.'

'What do you mean by that?'

'Oh, you'll see in just a few moments,' Maya said as she knocked on the apartment door they had been walking to. The door opened to reveal a woman with long dark hair who looked at them cautiously through the locked door chain.

Maya smiled pleasantly, drew one of her knives and cut apart the chain. The woman stumbled back as Maya opened the door with surprising delicacy. Further inside the cramped apartment was a small girl with pigtails and a beady-eyed little boy clutching each other.

'You can kill me, but please don't kill my children! Spare them, I beg you!' the woman pleaded as she fell to her knees, placing herself between Maya and her children.

Still smiling, Maya knelt to the woman and looked into her eyes.

'Don't worry. I won't do a thing,' Maya said, before she sprung up, walked to the wall at the far end of the apartment and placed her back against it. 'Alright, Colt, kill them all.'

'What?' Colt blinked.

'Wait! Please don't! We haven't done anything wrong! Please!'

'Our job today is to eradicate these three homunculi, so that's what you're going to do to prove yourself,' Maya explained. Her smile had not budged.

'But these are weak children. They are a threat to no one,' Colt said.

'That's right. My children have never done anything bad to humans. Please, I beg you, spare them!' the woman begged, still on the floor.

'Colt, this is the reality of our profession. Ninety-nine-point-nine percent of our jobs will be like this since the majority of homunculi are honestly quite weak and powerless. The high death rate of hunters comes from the immense power of an incredible few homunculi, or from a homunculus who gets the drop on some dumbass. Most of the homunculi are like these three here,' Maya explained with a sigh.

'So then, why kill these weak homunculi?'

'That's easy. People are stupid. They fear things they don't understand. They want comfort and reassurance that those things can't hurt or bother them. We're kind of like pest control. Most homunculi, like most pests, don't put your life in danger, they're just annoying or mildly frightening. We kill them to give peace of mind to stupid people, that's all it is. We kill them so the public can go to bed soundly.' Maya shrugged.

Colt was silent, unmoving.

Damn, looks like he's no good.

'See? Killing us is foolish. Young man, please—' The woman never finished her sentence. Colt's blade sliced through her neck and swiftly decapitated her children before any of them could realise what was happening.

'So you are fit for this job!' Maya said as she went

to pat him on the back, only to notice his heavy breathing.

'Are you alright? Did it bother you?'

'No, I simply want to remember this moment. This moment when their unending lives were given meaning. I want to remember the meaning of their deaths and carry it with me,' Colt said, his voice shook, and his hands trembled.

'So then, could you do it again?'

Colt gulped, closed his eyes and took a deep breath.

'Yes. When the old man died, I realised that death gives us meaning. I will keep killing to provide those who lost their humanity with meaning.' Colt met Maya's gaze.

Wow, his eyes are steeled. It's kinda scary... I guess I got a good one this time.

'Sounds good. You're certainly wild enough for this profession,' Maya chuckled.

Shin wiped away the tear rolling down his cheek. Although he felt fondness toward Maya and Colt, Shin could not help but feel immense sadness on their behalf.

Maya had told him of that killing simply in passing. She had not seen anything wrong with it. Instead, she smiled as she told the story.

Next Chapter Preview:

Endless

When does killing end?
When blades are sheathed or broken?
Nay, tis eternal

Chapter 6: Lamb Yiros

'So tender and juicy! It's like I've died and gone to meat heaven,' Maya bellowed, drawing the attention of everyone within the small establishment.

'While I do not share your idiotic level of adoration, it is incredibly well-executed. The lamb is tender and generous, elevated by the yoghurt garlic sauce. The vegetables add further texture and the flatbread simply completes it,' Colt said.

'Yeah! It's so good, right? Man, I'm glad we came here today.'

'It is good, but could you please be quiet? Everyone is staring at us,' Colt hissed.

'C'mon, our job is supposed to be near here, so this way we can easily check, right?' Maya smirked.

'Sometimes, your idiocy does make sense,' Colt conceded with a sigh.

Maya raised the blank screen of her phone. None of the people behind them appeared in its reflection.

'See? That was helpful, right?'

'Yes, it certainly was. Now I do not have to worry about catching human patrons in the chaos,' Colt conceded as he drew his sword.

Maya turned toward the bench where the three members of the serving staff were working.

'Hey, sorry, but we're going to make some mess. Don't worry though, a team will come clean it up later. Besides, you'll get some nice hush-hush money.' Maya gave a thumbs up. Before the stunned staff could respond, Maya sliced open the throats of the two patrons directly behind her.

Colt followed suit by removing the heads of the three who were seated on the same bench in one neat sweep. What followed next was chaos. The remaining patrons ran in all directions, screaming and bellowing for their lives. The five that headed toward the entrance were intercepted by Maya. Her blades reduced them all to shredded pieces of flesh that slopped to the floor.

'It's easy when you don't have to hold back,' Maya remarked with a whistle. Meanwhile, a group of six homunculi were attempting to run through the door to the kitchen, hoping to escape through the back door. A hope that was swiftly dashed when Colt's sword cut five of them apart, leaving one man looking on in despair at the pitiless boy before him.

'You little bastard! You killed them all! For what?! Damn you!' he screamed as he desperately charged Colt, who raised his sword for another clean kill. However, as his blade began to descend Colt realised it would not strike in time.

He is too fast! Our blows will be mutual... I will... die...

In that instant Colt froze, unable to act, unable to think. Everything ceased for Colt, everything except the thunderous beat of his heart. Then, Maya threw a knife at the man. It pierced his forehead and lodged itself within the man's brain. His attempt at revenge ended as his body fell to the floor. Maya walked to the man, knelt by his body and pulled the knife from the corpse with a grunt.

'Hey, what happened there?'

'I...' Colt was unable to give an answer.

Why could I not move? Was that fear? Was I re-

ally afraid? But I... I thought that I...

'Um, you're spacing out. Is every—'

'I am fine, just frustrated,' Colt answered swiftly as he turned away from Maya.

'Are you sure?'

'Yes'

'If you say so, but if you want to talk, you can come to me. I'll listen, I promise.'

'Right...' Colt whispered, unable to truly hear Maya's words.

Next Chapter Preview:

Rain

What Was It?

What was it I felt?
The girl makes me confront it
The answer with rain

Apart

I love the soft rain
No one else feels the same way
I face their anger

Chapter 7: Milk Tea and Cheesecake, Iced Coffee and Banoffee Cake Part 1

The cheesecake was soft, sweet and fluffy. It was accompanied by a comfortingly gentle milk tea, the warmth of which melted away the cold from the rain outside. Colt softly exhaled. It had been an excellent way to unwind from a day of work.

'Phew! So good,' Maya loudly exhaled after she scoffed down her banoffee cake and slurped down the last of her iced coffee. 'The desserts are always great here, but I don't get why you get tea. Iced coffee is always the perfect accompaniment to desserts.' Maya pointed her fork at Colt.

'I do not like coffee. It is far too bitter. Besides, tea is better for relaxation because it does not have nearly as much caffeine as that does,' Colt sighed as he pointed toward Maya's empty cup.

'Aw, that's so cute. You've still got your kiddie sweet tooth.'

'Shut up. I like what I like.'

'Hey, I guess I can't argue with that. That's not a bad outlook, especially for someone so logical.' Maya smirked.

'Thank you, I suppose.'

'I suppose you're welcome. Anyway, what are you doing next? Want to do some shopping and have dinner at my place? I got some lamb sausages on sale. I was thinking I'd cook them up with some steamed vegetables, with rye bread and garlic butter on the side.'

'No, I want to head home while I am still relaxed and get in some reading. I want to meditate a little bit.'

Damn, I was looking forward to it. Ah well... Maya thought with a sigh.

'Alright then, I guess I'll stay here and enjoy an after-work cigarette.'

'How can you smoke after eating tasty food? Would it not utterly ruin the flavours?'

'Poor Colt, still not able to grasp the adult world.' Maya patted Colt's shoulder.

'Fool, there is nothing adult about such an irrational vice. You should quit. It would be good for your body.'

'Wait, I thought you didn't care what smoking does to me. Why do you want me to quit?'

'It is just... If you were to die from that stupid vice... The meaning of a death like that would be too sad,' Colt nearly whispered. Maya was stunned for a moment.

Oh, so this is him, the real him behind all his philosophical bullshit... It's nice.

'Alright, maybe I'll try and quit then.'

'Truly?' Colt perked up.

'Sure, just let me have one smoke today.'

'You truly are hopeless,' Colt sighed.

'Hey, can't blame a girl for wanting one last puff, right? But seriously, I'll try and quit after that.'

'I will hold you to that.'

Why was I so invested in Maya quitting? A sad death? Were those truly my own words?

The rain pattered against Colt's umbrella, his thoughts lost in the clouds.

I do not understand. Death itself is the meaning of life. Why would the manner of death matter? All deaths lead to the same place. So then why did I react that way? It does not make sense...

His footsteps splashed in puddles as he walked onto a bridge, its stone body hanging over a bellowing river. Colt stopped as he noticed a girl standing on the railing. Tears ran down her face, mixing with the rain, as she stared into the dark river below.

She is going to jump.

Colt felt himself speed up. The image of the girl's crying face burned into his mind.

This is not...

He remembered finding the old man's corpse lumped comfortably in that old creaky chair. A smile was upon the old man's face.

This is not what death should be!

The girl turned toward the rapid footsteps approaching her.

'Stay away! You can't—'

'I will not stop you. If you truly want to die here, do so. However, I want you to ask yourself if this is what you truly want. Is dying here the meaning you want to leave behind? Are there still things you want to achieve? Or understand? Only by resolving these things can we leave this world with meaning that will satisfy ourselves and others,' Colt spoke softly. The woman was silent. Colt handed her his umbrella. 'It is all up to you. Decide your own meaning.' Colt continued onward through the rain.

I think I understand it more, that living is also important to meaning. The old man's death had such a powerful meaning because of the time I spent with him, because of his long satisfying life. His smile

showed me that, but that girl's tears showed a meaning of sadness and loneliness. Living... Just in living
itself, there is meaning... Perhaps just as much as
death, because the meaning of death is shaped by
the kinds of lives we live. That is why I want Maya to
live a long time. I want her death to be just as good
as the old man's, because she has great meaning in
my life. Then... Is death the most important thing?
Or is life? Or are both intertwined?

Colt stopped, sopping wet, before his apartment
building.

Maya, what is it that I—

His thoughts were interrupted when he noticed
an unfamiliar woman standing at the entrance to the
building. Her long mandarin hair draped to her shoulders. Her emerald eyes and lips were unmoving, her
suit was drenched. Colt felt a shiver down his spine.

'Who are you?' Colt asked cautiously as he reached
for his blade.

'I was waiting for you. My name is...'

Maya took in one last satisfying puff of her cigarette.

*This is the last one. I'm never smoking again.
Wait, why did I tell him I would quit? Why am I resolving to quit? Smoking is a part of my ordinary life.
It's something I'd fight and kill for. So then... Why
would I say that?*

'Hey, you,' a sharp feminine voice interrupted Maya's thoughts.

'Yes?' Maya answered as she turned to the petite
woman with short sandy hair and squinted hazel eyes.
The woman lifted her phone and revealed a photo-
graph of a dark-haired young man.

I remember him. That droopy homunculus I took

out the day I had Banh Mi for lunch. Man, that was good. I should have that again.

'Recognise this guy?'

'Yeah, he was a homunculus so I killed him.' Maya nodded.

The woman went to slap Maya, but Maya reflexively bent backward and evaded it.

'That was my boyfriend! He never killed anyone! Did he even fight back?' the woman cried.

Maya held out her phone, the woman reflected in the blank screen. *Huh, just a regular person that dated a homunculus. Weird, but at least I don't have to do any sudden work,* she thought.

'Nope, he didn't fight back at all,' Maya replied as she put her phone back in her pocket.

'How could you kill him?! What did he do to you?'

'I killed him because it's my job.' Maya shrugged.

'Heartless bitch. Don't you care about the suffering you cause?'

'Not really.'

'Don't you have people you care about more than anything. Can't you understand the pain? Answer me!' The woman's words burnt with anger and sorrow. A name burst into Maya's mind.

Colt.

'Yeah, I do. There's someone I care about more than anything.'

Colt is the most important part of my ordinary life. So much so that I'm willing to throw away other parts of it. That's why I'm willing to compromise, to change things in my life I would ordinarily fight, kill and die for. Because Colt... He...

'I get it! Thank you! I need to tell him!' Maya said with a grin, tightly grasping the woman's shoulders.

'What?' said the baffled woman.

Maya swiftly dashed away.

Colt... I... I need to tell you!

The woman fell backward, dazed and unable to process the events that had just occurred.

'What the hell? What was with her?' the woman whispered as she watched Maya run out of sight.

Next Chapter Preview:

Soon

I will soon see death
A battle between strong wills
What death will I see?

Chapter 8: Milk Tea and Cheesecake, Iced Coffee and Banoffee Cake Part 2

'Carla. I have given you my name as a formality. My teacher told me to always give my name before I take life. Now I can kill you as retribution for all of my brethren you have taken away,' the scarlet-haired woman uttered.

Colt brought out his blade. Carla swiftly closed the gap between them and grasped Colt's arm in one hand. With a light pull, Carla broke his arm with a soft snap.

Colt cursed as his arm went limp. His blade began to fall toward the ground. Before it could, he swiftly grasped it with his other hand and swung it toward Carla's neck.

Carla sighed. She easily caught the blade with a clap of her palms. 'This is your retribution. I will entrench you in the very despair you bestowed upon the helpless ones you slaughtered without remorse,' Carla uttered as she pushed her hands together. The blade shattered and clattered to the ground in fragments. Colt was unable to move, unable to speak, unable to do anything.

I understand. I understand it all. I was wrong. It

was all a lie. The old man's death made me sad, so I gave the death itself meaning. Taking the lives of others was painful, so I veiled it behind some philosophy. It was all just a lie I was stupidly ignorant of. A way to hide my pain, to live with what I have done! It is all so pathetic. This woman is right. I do deserve to face despair and die horribly. I am a hypocrite, spouting nonsense about death, but afraid of my own. I am such trash! I deserve this...

Carla stood above the frozen Colt. She raised her arm.

But I do not want to die yet! In reality, living itself creates its own meaning. That is the meaning we undertake in death, the one we shaped by our lives, that others hold onto after we die. Living is more than just the prelude to death! Death alone does not give us meaning! To keep living is the only way to find meaning for ourselves! I... I want to see that for myself. I want to keep living. I want to keep eating good food. I want to keep debating philosophy! I want to better understand this world. And I... I want to keep spending every day with Maya. I want to keep living with her. I do not want to die without her beside me at least. No, I do not want to die at all. I want to live!

Carla thrusted her arm toward Colt. He closed his eyes. His body fell backward. His eyes burst open.

I am alive! But how?

Carla was a good metre in front of him. Maya stood between them, her back turned to him.

'Just stay right there. I'll take care of this bitch,' Maya's warm upbeat voice told him. Colt smiled as tears rolled down his face until he noticed Maya's severed arm right next to him.

Blood spurted from Maya's now empty shoulder socket.

'Damn, that makes things hard.' Maya clicked her tongue as she drew a knife with her remaining left hand. Carla looked at her quizzically.

'Doesn't that hurt? Why are you unfazed?'

'Nah, it's nothing really. Well, nothing compared to what losing the most important part of my ordinary life would be. So, I'm just going to grin and bear it as I tear you apart.' Maya rushed toward Carla.

'I see... You hunters are dangerous.' Carla switched her stance and let loose with a volley of attacks. Maya weaved forward, barely avoiding death as she accumulated nail slashes that spilled her blood across the ground. Carla's crimson nails cut sharper than blades. With each strike, Maya had evaded death with a graze. Carla could easily tear apart Maya's flesh and bones if a slice truly landed. Despite this imminent doom, the overpowered enemy before her and blood that pooled from her body, Maya was smiling.

I just came here to tell Colt about my realisation. I needed to tell him no matter what. Glad I had that urge. If I didn't, he'd be dead. Thank God he's still alive.

Carla swept for Maya's head. Maya ducked and then cut the tendons in Carla's legs. Carla buckled backward and cursed. Maya seized her chance, leapt up and moved to take out Carla.

I'm probably about to die. I've lost a fair bit of blood. But... I'm fine with that? This ordinary life I've defended for so long... Am I honestly throwing it away?

'Maya, look out!' Colt screamed.

With that warning Maya sidestepped away from Carla's powerful punch, one that would have smashed Maya's skull. Instead, Carla's other hand pierced through Maya's gut. Maya coughed up blood. Her breath became sharp. However, there was a smile on her face.

Of course I am! If Colt died, what kind of ordinary life would it be? Having lunch, arguing or even just walking wouldn't be anywhere near as fun without him. He's special to me, so I'm going to die for him! I'm going to kill this bitch and protect him! It's natural after all, to protect the ordinary life where I belong, and the precious people that make it. That's something I'd massacre every other person in the world to protect.

'You're smiling? What the hell are you? You're not human! You're a demon! A monster far worse than what any of us could be!' Carla screamed as she looked upon Maya's wide smile, punctuated by the blood that fell from the corners of her mouth.

Maya thrusted her blade into Carla's temple, then with a click of her tongue, she twisted the blade until a satisfying splat was heard. Life left Carla's eyes. Blood streamed down the handle of Maya's knife. Carla's corpse fell to the ground, blood pooling around her. Maya fell to her knees, her breathing sharp and short.

'Hey... Colt...' Maya spoke through pained wheezes, but she still smiled.

'Maya!' Colt screamed as he rushed to her.

'You're okay... I'm glad... But I wish... I could have... stayed with you and held you a little...'

'You can. I'm right here,' Colt said as he knelt beside Maya. He wrapped his arm around her and pressed against her body tightly.

'I'll stay with you. I'll embrace you. We can stay like this as long as you like. So please, stay here, Maya. Please don't go, Maya. Please just stay with me,' Colt whispered as he clutched her cold body.

Next Chapter Preview:

To The Next

Life and death,
Intertwined and yet separate
Revered and despised
Understood and yet endlessly questioned
What lies beyond them?
What answer is there for them?
Maya,
I think I see it now,
The path forward,
Beyond life and death

Final Chapter: Tokyo and Karaage Ramen

Yet again, Colt found himself in the graveyard, once more among the rows upon rows of graves that had once been their meeting place. His eyes were focused upon the grave before him, a large rectangular headstone with the name 'Maya Kanagawa' etched upon it, an eternal monument to their separation.

'Sorry, Maya. I had it backward. I will treasure my life. Thank you, you fool,' Colt whispered to her. Beside him, Grace knelt to place a bouquet upon the grave.

'I honestly thought she was too wild to die. Ever since I met Maya she never allowed anything to get in her way. Morals, ethics, laws, common sense. None of these things meant anything to her. That's why she was able to kill and live for so long. She didn't have the limitations that restrict and endanger anyone who considers themselves normal. Nevertheless, Maya was still just human. She had feelings like the rest of us. Almost everyone has someone they'd die for, so don't feel guilty for her death. One day, you might find yourself doing the same as her,' Grace said quietly. She put a cigarette in her mouth and lit it.

'I see,' Colt said without looking away from the grave.

Silence filled the air. Grace stood.

'Grace, would you be willing to answer a question

of mine?' Colt's voice softly punctured the silence.

'Sure. What is it you want me to answer?'

'Why did Maya have to die?'

'Because she had something to protect, that's just how it goes.'

'Then allow me to rephrase; why do we actually kill homunculi in the first place? What are homunculi?'

'Ah, what an excellent question. Homunculi are beings created by the scientist Fraulein Faust in the nineteenth century. Faust created them to fight demons. Apparently, Faust wanted the homunculi to fight in the stead of the weaker Exorcists to prevent them from being killed, but the homunculi ended up being weak for the most part. The Order wanted them eradicated but Faust wanted to protect them. Hence, they came to an agreement which included that only regular suckers like us could enforce population control. I guess the answer is that hunters and homunculi are both just people, killing them is simply our role to maintain the balance established between Faust and the Order. Maya died because she had a job to do and something to protect.'

'I see. We truly are the ones who deserve death and suffering.' Colt nodded stiffly.

Grace chuckled. 'Now that I've answered your question, let me ask you my own. After all you've been through, now that you know the complete truth behind what you've been doing, what are you going to do now?'

'I will keep doing this work.'

'Oh? What made you decide that? I would have thought you would want to quit. I mean, wouldn't you prefer to be a noble Exorcist? Or maybe just a good, normal person?'

'I do not know what else I can do with my life. I have already taken so many lives that I cannot turn away from this life. I cannot ever become a truly good person. I must keep going upon this path. I want to see this life through... Actually, I am not sure if that is the whole truth. I cannot go elsewhere, so I am stuck here really. I cannot say if that is another lie I'm telling myself or the honest truth. All I can say is I cannot change to a supposed noble profession. I simply have to keep walking through the absurdity of this profession.' Colt turned away from Maya's grave to look Grace in the eye. Grace stared back into Colt's steeled eyes. She chuckled.

'Is that so? Good choice. I think Maya would approve. One day we should reminisce about her, over some nice long smokes.'

'That sounds fine, but I hate cigarettes. There is nothing fouler in this world.'

'How about I introduce you to your new partner then? Hey, you can come out now,' Grace called out.

A girl with a mandarin-coloured fringe and dark green eyes in a neat suit came out from behind the rows of graves.

'It's you, the girl from the bridge,' Colt said as the girl walked up to him and held out an umbrella.

'This is yours,' said the girl.

'Oh, thank you,' Colt said, taking the umbrella.

'Her name is Judy Limes. She asked specifically to be your partner,' Grace said.

'Is that right?' Colt asked.

'Your words made me think about it and I decided not to die. But I had no clue what I should do with my life. I had no direction as to where I could find that meaning you spoke of. So, I went looking for you, and thanks to Grace, here I am,' Judy explained.

'This profession is not a clean one. We make mountains of corpses. We kill only a few guilty. We mostly cut down the innocent. You could also die. All these graves are our co-workers who have gone before us. This one here was my last partner, she was... incredibly special and was stupidly strong, but even she died. Are you sure you can handle that?' Colt's eyes burned into Judy's.

'Yes! I just want to find my own meaning. I don't care about what I do to find it. Morals and ethics can go to hell, they don't mean a damn thing,' Judy said instantly. Colt chuckled.

'I like you. You remind me of her. You are wildly determined beyond all measure. I will take you on. Alright, Grace, we are off.' Colt turned and began to walk away.

'Take care,' Grace said with an exhale of smoke and a small wave.

'Um, where are we going?' Judy asked as she quickly followed Colt.

'It's Monday. We're going to get ramen,' Colt answered without looking back.

'But—'

'Did you genuinely think cold-hearted killers do not have to eat? Eating is massively important. You need to have the strength to fight intense battles. Good filling meals are a must in this profession,' Colt said.

Damn, I am starting to sound like you. Perhaps... That is not a bad thing. But I am never going to smoke.

'Oh, I get it. But, um, you said ramen, right?'

'I did.'

'Well, do they have any ramen with that nice Japanese-style fried chicken?'

Colt stopped in his tracks. He put a finger to his chin and paused for a good few moments.

'Actually, I think there is karaage ramen,' Colt said.

'Great! I'm going to have that then!'

'Glad you understand at least.' Colt smirked.

The absurd road of killing stretched onward. The two merrily marched forward without a care.

RACHEL WALKER AND THE MECHANISM OF TRUTH

Chapter 1: Little Red-Haired Busybody

It has been two whole weeks, and yet, Jill's death still freshly occupies my mind.

I did not see her die. I did not see her corpse, because her family opted to have a closed-casket funeral. Despite that, whenever I close my eyes, Jill appears before me. I see her warm smile. I hear her sweet laugh and feel her hand playfully ruffling through my hair.

Those fond memories bring forth sorrow, sorrow for the days Jill will now never see, sorrow for how she will no longer warmly tease or encourage me. These sorrows almost make me burst into tears, tears that would overflow a whole nation. However, my sorrow is managed by my refusal to accept this state of being. I grip my navy blue skirt tightly, my eyes fixating upon it as my determination takes over.

Jill died saving her boyfriend's life. As he began falling into the abyss she pulled him back, only for her to fall instead, only for her to die. That's the story, at least.

The police concluded it was a tragic accident and released the boyfriend. Although it was reported that Jill had skin and blood under her fingernails, the police found it was not his blood and he had no scratches anywhere on his body. Even so, I cannot release that fact from my mind. That blood had to have come from somewhere and her boyfriend's presence was far too convenient and coincidental in every possible regard.

Something is missing. Something does not fit. Perhaps it is merely my own need to find closure. Perhaps it is my mechanism for processing the world.

Last week, I could seldom walk without tears streaming down my face. As though I was a machine without maintenance, I was on the verge of falling to pieces upon the unforgiving concrete. Yet, the lingering inconsistencies and my single goal to find their resolution maintain my fragile self.

'Uh, Rachel? What do you think? Is the proposal for the new computer booking rotation okay to you?' The secretary's voice brings my gaze up into the SRC room.

The others all stare into me. Those quivering eyes, so fragile, yet devoid of anything that could be beauty. I find myself reminded of why I submerged myself in my thoughts. These people merely spill empty platitudes as they drearily nod to unattainable ideals. I joined the SRC out of a passion to do the right thing, a passion that allowed me to become president in year eleven over my seniors. However, I was swiftly directed to the reality that the SRC simply existed to hold meaningless meetings. Nothing will change. Nothing will be improved. They will simply spill empty words and then disperse with self-serving smiles. It still disgusts me to no end. Hence, I sought to make change by enforcing rules, confronting bullies, and lecturing rule breakers. Because of this, combined with my red ponytail and one hundred fifty-centimetre height, I was labelled as the 'Little Red-Haired Busybody'. I had viewed the label with complete indifference until Jill mentioned it.

'It's cool, Rachel. You probably don't care, but I

think you should be proud of it. That name shows your determination and ultra-strong sense of justice has merit,' Jill had told me, beaming. The label was thus etched upon my soul with boundless pride. Even in this very instant, I feel that I must uphold that namesake. I have to find the truth behind Jill's death, to answer that which lies a mystery. I look to the secretary sharply. She slightly lowers her gaze.

'I approve, timekeeper. Record that in minutes. Does anyone have anything else to discuss?' I ask.

'N-no.' The secretary shakes her head.

'Alright, I now end this week's meeting.' I swiftly stand and walk out of the room, feeling the eyes of the other student council members following me.

Fools. Feel content doing nothing but biting your thumbs. I am going to actually do something. I will find the truth.

As I walk out of the door, I notice a boy in uniform kneeling beside it. At the sight of me he jumps to his feet energetically. He has circular glasses upon his playful hazel eyes and mid-length sharp blonde hair.

'Lucien, what can I do for you?' I ask.

'Actually, it's the opposite, Miss Prez,' Lucien chuckles.

'Call me Rachel. Honestly, how annoying. But I do not think you can help me with—'

'Finding details on Jill's death? C'mon, Miss Prez, I'm one of your very, very, very few friends. I know you pretty damn well. You're probably going to need some help with this, help I can provide with my social skills and my impressive online information gathering skills.' Lucien puffs out his chest.

I sigh. Lucien honestly has a point I cannot easily refute. I will most likely need his help. I know doing this alone will be difficult and my abrasive integrations will not always help with information gathering. I smirk. I must concede I have been blessed with rather good friends.

All the more reason I have to do this, for the great friend Jill was.

'Alright, please help me.'

'That's what I'm talking about! So, what now?'

'Jill never told me who her boyfriend was, so I'll start by asking about the identity of her boyfriend.'

'Hold on, you didn't know who he was?'

'I was a bit too judgmental in the past, so Jill was secretive and never really shared with me.' A pang of guilt falls into my words, my heart stings a bit.

'Well... How about Jill's other friends? Surely someone would know who her boyfriend was.'

'Despite the gossip about her death, most everyone else in the school is also in the dark, especially since the police did not release his identity.' This clearly demonstrates how my judgement hurt Jill. Surely, if her other friends knew, they would have gossiped and his identity would be well known throughout the school.

'Rachel... You know, you shouldn't stress so much about the past. So, how about we focus on right now. Like, where do you think we should start?' Lucien replies, clearly trying to get me to focus away from my guilt. I suppose he has always been able to see right through me. I feel a bit better, as though I can take one more step forward. I focus on the present, the shadow of the past seeps behind me for the time being.

'I was thinking that if we talk to Jill's other friends, we might at the very least get a lead.'

'Nice! Let's go, Miss Prez!'

'I know it's pointless, but can you not call me that?'

'Nope!'

Web

Fall deeper yet more
Become entrapped in this web
You the fateful four

Chapter 2: Love Life

We stand outside the senior building, rerunning over what the few pieces of information we have gathered. The rusty colour bricks of the old building stood timelessly over us. A few students walked by on the grey stone pathway, consumed by their own chatter. Despite my best efforts, this investigation has yet to bear any fruit. Lucien and I have talked with eight of Jill's friends. No one knew the identity of her boyfriend. Three girls pass by, two gazing at their phones, while the other twirls her hazel bangs and mumbles to herself. I pull my attention away from my surroundings and back to my investigation. As I suspected. It appears Jill was a secretive person when it came to her love life, even with her friends. Hence, as we repeat the pattern with the ninth friend—Chloe Goods—I cannot help but fade into my thoughts, especially since the difficulty we face in this investigation, is entirely my fault in the first place.

Now that I think about it, Jill was always impulsive and devoid of caution when it came to relationships. She would date anyone who caught her eye, without any hesitation toward if they were good people or if they would take advantage of her, despite my lectures. Over and over, I would tell her the importance of restraint and that she should be cautious of others. I just wanted to protect her, my overly judgemental spiels drove Jill to stop telling her friends about her romantic relationships. I told myself that she had taken my advice, that I did not need to press her any longer. But that was just me lying to myself. Jill had simply closed that part of herself off from her friends. I should have supported her. I should have lent her my shoulder. I should have done something else. I should have done anything else. Instead, I simply continued as if things were normal. Everything was normal otherwise, so I never thought to apologise nor reconcile with Jill. I did not reach out because I could not see anything amiss. Then Jill died. Had I done something or been more supportive things might be different, she might still... Damn... Now I can never apologise... I can never hear her voice again...

I feel tears forming in the edges of my eyes.

'Are you okay?' A boy's surprisingly soft voice draws me outside of my thoughts. Back within reality, I turn to see a boy of striking normalcy approach me from my left, stopping his walk by to check on my evidently sad state. Short black hair, medium height, clean face and dark eyes. There is nothing about his physical features that stands out as unusual. However, there is something about him that compels me to be honest.

'Actually... I suppose I am not,' I answer.

What am I doing? I don't know this boy.

'Oh, do you want to talk? Sorry, I know that's weird... I mean, I just started talking to you out of nowhere, but I... couldn't leave you be, I guess. I mean, you look like you're about to cry,' the boy stammers.

I believe I have a part of an answer as to why I was drawn to this boy. This stranger is genuinely offering his hand in comfort simply because he could not turn away from me. I wipe away my budding tears.

My initial assumption about this boy was wrong...

Perhaps it is wrong to say he is simply normal, rather, his normality is...

'I don't know who her boyfriend was, but I know someone who does,' Chloe's words slam the train of my thoughts into the station called reality.

'Tell me who it is,' I say, perhaps too strongly.

'Her name is Michelle Lillico. She's pretty popular among us girls—and even some of the boys—because of her status as a "Love Meister". Not that you would know about that—Oh! Sorry!'

'No, it's fine. Please continue.'

'Michelle gives great love advice, so Jill would speak with her quite a bit. You can find her at the benches out near the tennis court,' Chloe explains.

'Thank you,' I say with gratitude.

I turn back to the boy. My mind is no longer focused on him. My goal has overtaken my curiosity toward him. However, I still feel as though I must grant him some words in reciprocation for his concern.

'I will be fine, but thank you. May I have your name?'

'It's Paul. Don't worry too much,' Paul chuckles.

'No, you helped me greatly, Paul. I feel a little bit stronger now,' I say with a small smile.

I race toward the tennis court. Lucien swiftly follows.

I may have failed you in life, Jill, but I can atone by finding the answer to your death.

Sitting upon a metal table, we see a slender girl with wavy hair, who I presume is Michelle Lillico. She smirks as we approach her, and the three black freckles on her cheeks bob upward as her inquisitive dark eyes lock onto us. She waves casually, revealing pink fingernails and a scrunchy wrapped around her wrist.

'Well, well. I never thought the SRC president herself would pay me a visit. How delightful. So, are they a boy, a girl or neither? Or maybe you're here because you want to get with the cutie you brought with you? Or is he here to ask about someone and you're escorting him? Or maybe you two want me to play matchmaker and speed your dormant feelings along?' Michelle rambles. I don't even begin to know how to answer.

'Honestly, I'd love any excuse to talk to a hottie like you, but Miss Prez here wants to ask you something. I'm just here to help her out.' Lucien shrugs with a smirk. I sigh inwardly, maintaining my poker face.

Lucien is indeed correct about me needing his help. There is no conceivable way I could handle those questions. Matters of love are far beyond my depth.

'Oh? Then lay it on me. There is nothing the Love Meister can't answer.' Michelle clicks her tongue.

'Then I will get right to the point. I want you to tell me the identity of Jill's boyfriend,' I demand.

Michelle's face hardens. 'Sorry, but that's something I actually can't answer. When it comes to love, you can't just blurt out things people tell you in confidence. Even if they're dead, you can't spill anything.'

'Please, I have to know.'

'Why is that?'

'Because I have to find the truth.'

'Why? Haven't the police already done that? Why do you need to solve something that's already taken care of?'

'I have to. Something is bothering me about it. I cannot leave it alone. When she was alive, I could have asked Jill, but I did not. I need to find those answers.

I have to.' I grip my skirt. The words that spilled out of me were honest. They hurt as they passed through my mouth. As I spoke, I wished I could shut my mouth and keep all that buried within the darkest recesses of myself. I grip tighter, for I know that the words had to leave my mouth, I had to speak them.

All I have to do is keep going. I have to keep moving forward.

Michelle sighs.

'His name is Laurence Jewel,' she concedes.

'Thank you so much,' I breathe with a sigh of relief.

'Actually, Jill was going to introduce you to him before she died. She told me she wanted to bury the hatchet and to stop avoiding the subject of dating. So, I was just doing Jill a favour I owed her,' Michelle nearly whispers.

A torrent of emotions crashes together in the coalescing river inside of me.

'Thank you.' I bite my lip to hold back my sobs. As Lucien and I walk away I come close to crying again. Lucien simply places his hand on my shoulder, bringing me comfort and allowing me to slowly regain myself.

'Lucien, do you know anything about Laurence?' I finally sputter out.

'Not much, but there are some guys I know quite well I can ask about him.'

'Please do. I doubt they will want me around, So I will leave it to you,' I say.

'Alrighty then. I'll call you later with the deets.'

Alone in the long halls, Jill calls my name. I turn to find her smiling at me. She stands on her tiptoes, her arms held behind her back.

'Jill, is that really you? Jill I—'

Jill laughs and bobs backward, moving away from me. I have to follow. I have to speak to her. I have to, more than anything else. I follow her, having to run as she swiftly picks up the pace. I chase after her as she continues her backward motion, neatly clacking up the stairs in a diagonal jumping motion. Jill chuckles, opening a door and leaping away for me.

My heart fills with dread. I know what awaits outside that door. I have to go to her. I have to stop it. This time I have to save her.

I burst through the door, panting as I brace myself. Before me, I see Jill standing on the balcony with the easily climbable railing. Jill smiles at me. I pause and stand, relieved. Then a dark figure, cloaked in shadow, throws Jill off the balcony. I lurch forward and outstretch my hand to grab her. Jill reaches out to me.

I will save you! I will reach you! Hold on! I—

The vibration of my phone jolts me from my slumber. I sit up and take a moment, allowing reality to slowly return to me as I let out sharp breaths.

A dream... Damn! If only I had... No... It was merely a dream. Nothing I did there mattered.

I take a deep breath and shake my head free of the dream as I pick up my still-vibrating phone. Lucien is calling. I answer.

'Hello.'

'Geez, you sound super drowsy. Did I wake you up?'

'Do not worry about it.'

'Of course I'm going to worry. You haven't been sleeping well so you probably fell asleep right after you got home without meaning to, right?'

'How did you—'

'You suck at taking care of yourself.'

'I... cannot deny that.'

'You probably dreamed about Jill, right? I might have ripped you from a pleasant dream, or maybe I rescued you from a nightmare... No, I won't ask. Sorry. Try and sleep well later so you can set a good example, Miss Prez,' Lucien says.

Am I truly that predictable? Or does Lucien know me far too well? Regardless, I am grateful to have him as a friend. Explaining that dream would have been hard on me. Lucien is being considerate of my feelings, in his own way.

'Thank you.'

'Anyway, I have information on Laurence.'

'Tell me.'

'Well, according to the guys he's a bit of a wimp. He always avoids fights and cries whenever someone gets hurt. Sounds like a person who wouldn't hurt a fly, right? But that's where it gets interesting. Apparently, he panics at complete random, because he thinks that someone called "the Baneful Shade" is "standing before him".'

'The Baneful Shade?'

'Yeah, none of the guys know what that means exactly, but they say Laurence describes the Baneful Shade as a frightening black shadow that follows him everywhere.'

'So he has visual hallucinations?'

'Yeah, so he regularly sees Miss Humzy.'

'Thank you. That is supremely helpful.'

'No prob, but what'll you do next?'

'I will call Miss Humzy and arrange to have a word with her tomorrow.'

Love

Love from the bosom
Burning such a bright red hue
So very pretty

Chapter 3: Confessions of the Love Meister

I have to be honest about something. Despite being a self-proclaimed "Love Meister" I had not actually fallen in love until not too long ago. Sure, I had been attracted to and had fun with numerous boys and girls, but I'd never actually fallen in love. I'd never felt my heart tug and ache before. That was until I met Jill.

She had come to me for advice. Her ex-boyfriend was upset with her for breaking up with him out of the blue. It was then I fell in love for the very first time. It was as I gazed upon her long, silky gold hair, soft skin and gentle ocean eyes. It was as I listened to her tell me about her dilemma, to her friendly tone, to her musical laughter. My heartbeat was like a machine gun against my chest. It felt like there was a rabbit stuck in my throat. Even then, I think I did a pretty good job hiding it.

'You should just apologise like you mean it. Sure he'll still be upset, but this guy sounds like he's not the vengeful type. He's just annoyed you ditched him,' I said casually, despite everything going on inside me.

'Yeah, I'll apologise this afternoon. I probably hurt him a bit...' Jill sounded genuinely remorseful. I couldn't quite see why at the time.

'Good, then we can be a happy little couple.' I playfully chuckled. It was a standard joke I made all the time. Usually, it was greeted with amusement, confusion, or a sigh. I find that stupid jokes help alleviate the tension and worry with breakups. In this case, I was also using this joke to mask my real feelings.

'Hmm... Not a bad idea. You're really cute, Michelle. Would you go out with me?' Jill asked as she leaned into me. My cheeks had burned the brightest they had ever been. My heart nearly burst. I didn't expect Jill to seriously make a move on me, especially in such a nonchalant way.

'Um, well, okay...' was all I could manage to squeak out. It was another first, the first time I was at a loss in a relationship. She called me 'really cute'. I often feel flattered when people compliment my appearance, but this time swept me off my feet. In a matter of minutes, my previously playful and aloof self, had been hopelessly swept up into Jill. It was three blissful weeks, a total paradise of loving dates, shared laughter and heartfelt words. Then, it ended as all good things do.

'Thank you, Michelle. I loved our time together,' Jill told me one day. I knew what it meant. I nodded and smiled.

'Yeah, paradise is best kept short and sweet.' I used to actually believe that. After all, my stupid parents ended up loveless and divorced before I was even five. I thought relationships were best kept short, to avoid bickering and complications, not given the time to fizzle out or become bitter like my parent's marriage.

But when Jill broke up with me, I realised that wasn't entirely true. I wanted to stay with her, for as long as I could. From the depths of my heart, I wished I could stay with her forever. When I went home that day, I cried.

Even then, I wasn't really mad at Jill or held a grudge. We stayed friends. I could continue giving her love advice for all her new escapades and she'd spend time with me and listen to my stupid jokes. Honestly, I was happy she hadn't grown to hate me or abandoned me out of boredom. Especially because from our time together, I had grown to truly understand Jill.

I understood where that remorse from before came from. I understood that Jill didn't experience love in the typical sense. Jill was overflowing with love. She fell in love at the drop of a hat and wanted to experience it with all kinds of people. But Jill truly loved everyone she was in a relationship with, she just couldn't choose one person to have all of her love. So she decided to experience and share all the love she could with all the people she felt love towards. I kept hanging around her. I'll admit I was jealous of those others she shared her love with, but I was content. Then, things changed.

'Michelle... I'm in love, but this time... I... I think I need to stay with him...' Jill's eyes lowered as she whispered. I was stunned. It was the first time the always happy and bright Jill was so quiet. It took me a second for me to truly grasp the meaning of her words.

'You want to stay with this boy?'

'Yeah... I... Sorry, I don't know how to put it, but the thought of not being with him makes my heart tighten and I want to cry,' Jill said. Weirdly enough, all my jealousy melted away. I was happy for her. I was happy she experienced the same love I felt for her, even though it was directed at someone else.

'Alright then! I'll give you the greatest advice ever! Sit back and let the Love Meister do her thing,' I said with a grin.

'Michelle... Thank you.' The overwhelming bright smile on Jill's face was satisfying enough. It sounds cliché, but the fact that the person I loved was happy was enough for me. Then she died.

After Jill's death, I was a mess. I stayed home and sobbed. Eventually, I told myself Jill wouldn't want me to be such a wreck. If I had kept on like that her ghost probably would have turned up and tried to cheer me up.

So, I headed back to school with a cheerful outlook. It hurt a little. I was still sad, but I was able to keep it inside me. Having people ask me for love advice and talk to me normally helped.

Then, just a bit ago, the SRC president Rachel Walker showed up. She's a cute girl who's incredibly short with shining red hair, adorable freckles on her cheeks and sharp, inquisitive emerald eyes that would belong more on a grizzled old chain-smoking detective than a teenage girl. I knew of her of course, because of her reputation as 'The Little Red-Haired Busybody' but Jill had told me a lot about her as well. I knew they were truly great friends, and they had been that way since they were kids. Jill told me funny childhood stories, sad memories and warm bonding moments. In a weird way, I sort of felt like I knew her by proxy. That's why I felt so comfortable talking to Rachel, even over those painful subjects. It was nice to talk with her, to spark thoughts of Jill again.

As for why I told her about Laurence... Well...

I look upward. The afternoon sky has a slightly dark blue tinge as the frizzy clouds have faded a bit. I smile.

'Thanks for your advice, Michelle, but can I ask you to help with something a little different?' Jill had suddenly asked a few days before she died.

'Oh? Sure, what is it?'

'I'm going to tell Rachel about Laurence and I... I want to show her I've stopped dating around. I want to stop avoiding the subject. Every time I do it seems like I don't want her involved in that part of my life. But I do want her involved. I want to move forward. So, I'll tell her and introduce Laurence. After that, can I introduce you to Rachel? Could you help her out a little? Not with dating I mean. Rachel isn't interested and that's probably good for her right now. Instead, could you listen to her when she needs help more generally? Rachel has never had good people skills, and she's the type to hide her problems while she butts into other people's problems and solves them. So, could you be there for her?'

I chuckle at the memory.

'Jill, I'm not sure if what I did just now was what you asked me to do, but I did help her. I'm glad I could help her a little in your place. I think we could be friends. She seemed nice enough. Would that make you happy?' I say, still gazing upward, although I don't really need to receive an answer. I already know what Jill would say anyway.

Connection

Like a fine string thread
So easily cut apart
Yet endlessly strong

Chapter 4: A Chat

'Good morning, Rachel. I'm surprised you wanted to see me,' Miss Humzy greets me with a casual wave, tenderness glowing in her honey-tinted eyes.

'I'm surprised you were able to fit me in,' I remark. Miss Humzy is rather popular with my peers. I hear a lot of talk about how comforting and easy-going her counselling sessions are, particularly from a couple of juniors in the SRC.

Jill went to Miss Humzy on a whim after her parent's rough divorce. She came back after finding it helpful. In fact, Jill kept going back even after she came to terms with the divorce.

'It's just relaxing. She finds a way to connect with you. I know it's a little selfish, but it's nice,' Jill had told me with a sheepish grin.

'Nah, it was easy. Most of the students like seeing me either during the afternoon or in class time, so slotting you in the morning was actually really easy,' Miss Humzy said with a shrug. As she does, the sleeve of her long white jacket raises slightly. I notice an array of bandages on her arm.

She catches me staring.

'Oh, these? The work of various cats. I love them so much. Whenever I see one I want to pet it so badly. But they don't seem to share the sentiment. They rough me up before I can even touch them. I wonder if I did something bad in a previous life,' Miss Humzy chuckles, then sighs. I cannot help but feel bad for her. 'Where are my manners? Please sit down. We'll start whenever you're ready.'

She gestures toward a chair facing her. I sit and Miss Humzy pushes her square glasses up.

'So then, what did you want to talk about?'

'I want to know more about Laurence Jewel. Please tell me about him.' I look Miss Humzy right in the eyes. She sighs and leans back slightly.

'So, this is about Jill, right?'

'Yes.'

'You think Laurence did it?'

'I do.'

'Laurence didn't kill Jill. I assure you that he could not have.'

'What makes you so certain? Wasn't he having hallucinations? Clearly he was unwell.'

'You have done your research... I can't tell you very much, since I cannot break the confidentiality of my students, however, I will tell you the Baneful Shade was an illusion manifested from fear.'

'So this Baneful Shade was influencing him?'

'You misunderstand. The Baneful Shade was not another personality. It was a visual manifestation of Laurence's fears. It could not control him, nor have any sway over his actions. Instead, it loomed over him, as though a deep dark fear... One that must be hurting especially bad now...' Miss Humzy trails off as she lowers her gaze.

'Then what about the blood and skin? How did it get under Jill's fingernails?'

'It's alright, Rachel. Not everything has an answer. Just know, it's okay to be sad. It's okay for you to feel powerless and upset. You can cry and scream all you want. People tend to say that you have to keep it together, that you have to not fall apart, but there's nothing wrong with being sad. Just let it out,' Miss Humzy says softly. She stands.

'But I need to find the truth. I have to understand how—'

I'm shocked into silence as Miss Humzy embraces me.

'It's alright. You don't have to do anything. You don't have to prove yourself or find something to please the dead. You're not at fault. You can just cry. If anything, it's my cross to bear. I'm the one who failed.'

'I—'

'Poor thing, you've wrapped yourself further and further into this. It's okay. I'm here.' Miss Humzy pats my back. Her words are softer than a mother's. Tears fall from my eyes. I embrace Miss Humzy tightly.

'Thank you, but I cannot ever stop looking.'

I sniff as I wipe the last tears from my eyes. I open the door. Despite having cried, I feel so much better. It is as though the torrent of chaos within me has been calmed to a soft breeze.

'Thank you, Miss Humzy. That was nice,' I say.

'Of course. Feel free to come back anytime.' Miss Humzy gives me yet another warm smile.

'I might just do that.' I mean that truly. As I walk out of the door I wonder if I have felt this light since the day Jill died. For the first time in a while, I feel good.

'Please do. You have my interest now,' Miss Humzy warmly remarks. I nod to her as I shut the door behind me.

I can easily see why Jill was so comfortable with

Miss Humzy. It was so intimate and yet no boundaries were crossed. The experience helped me, at least just a bit.

'It's okay to be selfish. Do what you want,' Jill's words come back to me quickly.

Sorry, I guess I am still no good at that, Jill.

Quiet

A quiet girl now
Hiding herself behind lies
How truly boring

Chapter 5: The Eye of Death

As I walk the halls, I notice how quiet the place is. Later today, these halls will be packed with bodies, from which will bound a chorus of loud voices that will echo and stretch throughout the hall. Shoes and boots will squeak and clack as they push against the floors. Some will walk, some will run and some bodies will collide and cause chaotic outbursts of anger. Those are the halls I am used to seeing, but the one I am walking through now is almost alien. Silence and emptiness are things these halls hold for this short period of time, their true form, separate from the rabble I associate these halls with. A part of me finds it eerie, for an empty and silent hall is never associated with good things. However, a part of me enjoys the peace and quiet, broken only by the sounds I alone am making.

That is until I hear the laughter that is unmistakably Jill's from behind me. I freeze. A chill works its way up my spine. I slowly turn to face the laughter. I hold my breath as my heart hammers in my chest. I see a figure draped in black, walking toward me as the laughter continues.

'Jill? Is that you?' The figure ignores my question as it comes closer. 'Jill, I—'

My words are interrupted as the figure brandishes a knife. Without thinking, I start to run. The figure swiftly gives chase, the blade of the knife scraping against the wall, the metal scratches and claws away the wood.

That is a real knife! This is real! I could die! I will die!

Fear compels me to keep running. Without looking back, my legs burn ever forward without a notion of where they are even going.

I feel a hand grasp my shoulder. I find the figure standing above me. Out of desperation, I move to roundhouse kick the figure. The figure just easily grasps my leg and throws me to the ground. I slam into the hard floor. Waves of pain tear through me. I let out a guttural groan. I weakly turn to my side and attempt to raise myself. The directionless need to live still screams in my soul.

Too late!

The figure is standing above me. It raises the knife. In this moment, my fear washes away. Oddly enough, I find myself only left with regret, regret that I will never find the truth of Jill's death. I do not regret looking for the truth in the slightest.

Am I guilty for Jill's death? No... I do not feel guilty at all... So why do I regret not finding the truth?

'It's okay to be selfish. Do what you want,' Jill's words echo through my head, illuminating the truth behind my drive.

That's right. My want for the truth is selfish. I truly do want justice for Jill. I truly do want the truth to be revealed for her sake. But... I am also selfish. I want to find the truth for myself. No, I need to find the truth. Now that I have started looking for it, I have to find it no matter what. Not for a sense of justice, but because I am drawn to it for its own sake. I have to find it because that is what I want above all else. That is right. I must find the truth no matter what. For my selfish impulse, I have to live and find the truth. I have to. I have to reveal the truth!

'I am sorry, Jill. But I cannot die just yet. I have to find the truth behind your death. You told me to be more selfish, right? So please let me keep going!' I scream without thinking, desperately trying to reach my friend.

The figure stops. It stands as still as a sculpture for a few moments, then bolts away from me. I attempt to follow, but it is far too quick. It easily evades me and disappears. Out of breath, I kneel on the ground. I grasp my beating heart.

That is right... I need to keep going... No matter what, because I want to. Right, Jill? That got through to you, right?

Wrong

So terribly false
I could not have been more wrong
What a pretty truth

Chapter 6: The Account of an Ordinary Boy Part 1

My name is Paul Niles. I'm an incredibly ordinary person in pretty much every single way. I'm not exceedingly kind and I'm not secretly malicious. My grades are barely above average. I don't have any subject I struggle with or excel in. My teachers don't hate or love me. My peers don't go out of their way to pick on me or to hang out with me. I love my supportive parents. I squabble with my little sister, but I love her all the same. I don't have any particular talents or gifts. I don't have any glaring weaknesses or limitations either. In my free time, I read sci-fi books and play video games. Basically, my life is as boring and uninteresting as it could be. I can't see myself being important in anything, since there's nothing in my life that drives me to pursue a dream or goal and I'm way too boring to have the spotlight. I can imagine my classmates would be bored if they were forced to listen about my life.

A lot of people would see this as a bad thing. They'd want to stick out, to see themselves as the hero. Like the girl with the long hazel bangs in the courtyard just a few metres ahead of me, she's pacing back and forth, muttering into her phone about how she can't find a demon. I'm not one of those people. I like my life just the way it is, I don't need or want to

pretend it's something else. It's pleasant and peaceful. I'm honestly happy with this boring existence. As
a result, I've never wished or wanted anything weird,
exciting or life-changing to happen to me. Sadly,
the world seems to have an entirely different idea
regarding that.

I sit on the grass, reading a sci-fi book. The wind
blows through my hair and I look toward the direction
it comes from to the old school building. My eyes catch
sight of something through a window, a dark shadowy
figure. I can't quite make out what the hell it is, but
I can see something shimmer in its grasp. Even from
where I am, it is clear it's a weapon, probably a knife.

I blink in surprise. The figure remains. Most people
would probably assume it's an illusion, but before
thoughts like that can reason with me, I feel myself
running toward the school building. It's strange, like
my body is moving by itself. I can't figure it out. I
thought I was normal.

*I don't have time to think about that! That person
has a knife! I can't let someone get hurt!*

Maybe too normal. Wanting to stop a bad thing
from happening is tremendously normal, or maybe
my sense of what is 'normal' is entirely displaced.
Maybe, wanting to help people is entirely weird and
I'm a weirdo.

That doesn't matter right now! I have to hurry!

My thoughts stop as I burst through the door. I hear
a girl's voice call out about two flights of stairs above
me. I rush up the stairs, puffing as I reach the top. I
look around, the figure is nowhere in sight. Instead, I
see the SRC president kneeling and puffing.

I don't know her all that well. There would be
no reason to since I'm not an honour student nor a
delinquent. I just know her from her reputation and
because she was in my year nine English class. How-

ever, the other day she had a weird expression on her face. It was full of sadness, yet it was also detached, like she was very focused and cutting out everything unnecessary. I couldn't help but feel a deep sense of concern and ask if she was okay. It just slipped out of my mouth. It was far too weird. I don't even know why I pushed myself into her business.

But I'm here in front of her again. Is there something happening with her? Was that some sort of foreshadowing by the universe? Hm... That's... not important right now. I need to make sure she's unharmed.

'Are you okay?' I ask as I extend my hand out to Rachel. She takes it. I lift her to her feet.

'I'm alright. Wait... Paul? What are you doing here?' Rachel asks.

'Don't worry about that. Are you hurt?' I blurt out.

'You are a nice one. No, I am fine. Thank you for being there for me, again,' she says with a smile, but I'm not convinced.

'Look, uh, this might sound weird... But I was out on the grass reading and I saw a dark figure with a knife, so I—'

'You saw it?'

'Yes? Or at least, I'm pretty sure?'

'Interesting... That means it was real, not just something in my head. Maybe it is different from what I thought it was? I doubt a ghost like that would be so easily visible, especially one with a knife... Thinking it was a ghost was foolish... But then why did it stop after I screamed my feelings at it? It only attacked me after I started looking into... Yeah, maybe it is linked to that. In that case, I have to speak to *him*. Maybe he truly does have the key to this,' Rachel says more to herself than to me.

To be honest, I don't understand what most of

what she said was about. What I do understand is we both saw that figure, it attacked her, and she is in very real danger.

'Listen, a person tried to attack you, right? I think you should be more careful. Maybe stop whatever it is you're doing, or report it to the police?' I can't help myself. I have a knot in my stomach just thinking about her.

'I cannot do that yet. I just need a little bit more information and then I will have the truth.'

'I don't know what this is about, but it's not worth dying for, right?'

'Maybe, but I simply have to find the answer. For my own selfish reasons, I have to do this. Thanks for coming to help, but can you not mention this? Please forget about this. It is important to me.' Rachel smiles at me with such enthusiasm that I relent almost immediately.

'A-alright.'

'Thank you. You should probably head to your next class. It will begin soon.'

Our conversation started so weird, and she came off as kind and driven, the opposite of what I think most SRC members are like. But our conversation ends with a weirdly appropriate tone for the SRC President. Rachel walks away. I am left with my thoughts.

Idiot! You're going to let her do this? She's in danger! You can't give up.

Despite outwardly relenting to her, it seems the inside me is intent on keeping this going.

Why? Isn't this normal? Wouldn't it be weirder to abandon her?

I decide to help her. I honestly can't say why. I know I'm not in love with her, but I feel this need to help her no matter what. She is clearly in trouble, so I have to help her.

I guess that's all there is to it. I'm a weirdo after all.

After impatiently enduring school, I ask around in the afternoon. Rachel left school some time ago, so I can't confront her or tail her.

Dammit! I should have left earlier. Guess I'll just have to put my nose to the ground.

I find out Rachel had been trying to figure out the identity of Jill Helter's boyfriend. Apparently, Jill and Rachel were very close friends.

Is she trying to avenge Jill? Or trying to find a clue that's been missed? Hmm... Damn! I have no idea... But, it's clear she's put herself in a lot of danger. I need to hurry and find something else.

As I continue my leg work, I pick up a helpful little titbit. It seems like she paid the 'Love Meister' a visit. I recall that being the nickname of a girl who gives out love advice to anyone who asks, but I can't say if it's any good since I haven't tried it out myself. I head to the spot I'm told she usually hangs out in the afternoon. There, I find her sitting on a metal table, her right leg crossed over her left leg. Her right hand is wrapped around her right cheek and her left hand holds her phone, which she puts away when she sees me approach.

'Oh, hey, a boy. Got love problems? I can help, just come into my office.' She beckons me closer with her left hand lazily moving back and forth as a claw, she chuckles all the while.

'Well, I do have a serious problem, but it's not about love.'

'Oh? Not sure how much help I'll be, but feel free to ask.'

'This morning I saw a person in a dark figure with a knife. That person was attacking Rachel Walker. She didn't get hurt, but when I got there the attacker was gone and Rachel was talking about "asking him" and that "it wasn't in her head." To be honest, I have no clue what she was talking about, but I can't leave it be. I know it's not my business, but she's clearly in danger and I want to make sure she doesn't get hurt. So please, tell me what's going on. She asked you about something, right?' I blurt out.

'Damn! This is worse than I thought. I told her that Jill's boyfriend was Laurence Jewel. I thought she was just looking for closure, but she was clearly looking for something else. The attacker must be Jill's killer. This is very dangerous.' The Love Meister bites her bottom lip.

'So, Rachel's probably at Laurence's house trying to get answers. We should head there, or to her house,' I suggest.

'No, that will majorly backfire. It'll either look like we're stalkers or losing our minds. Rachel turned you away before. That's why you're talking to me, right? Instead, we should bring Rachel to us and a teacher I know we can trust.'

'What do you mean?'

'I'll give Miss Humzy a call and ask her to invite Rachel to a group session for people grieving Jill tomorrow morning. If she's with Laurence, she'll accept and probably ask him to come along. Then we can ask Rachel what the hell is going on and Miss Humzy can get the police involved.' Michelle smirks proudly as she speaks, a pride which I think is absolutely earned in this case given the ingenuity of her scheme.

'Let's do it.'

I won't let someone die. I'll do everything I can.

'Ok, I'll call Miss Humzy now.'

The Love Meister said she wasn't very good with things beside romance, but her plan is brilliant. Just what the hell kind of view does she have of herself? Although, I guess I'm not one to talk. I see myself as normal, but I'm definitely a weirdo, or at least more weird than I thought.

Two

Enter both of you
Please show me what lies beyond
Show me all your truths

Chapter 7: Reality

It is easy enough to get inside the house. I simply mention Jill's name and Laurence's mother opens the door and welcomes me inside. She tells me that it is good I am here, that I can help cheer him up a little. I venture she is under the impression we are friends, since we were both close to Jill. However, we have not met.

I stand before his door. I raise my hand to knock against it. My hand stops. It quivers.

There is no turning back. I have to find the truth. I resolved to, right? Then I have to keep going.

I take a breath, close my eyes and clench my hands into fists. I let out my breath, slowly open my eyes and relax my hands. I softly rap against the door with the back of my hand.

'My name is Rachel Walker and I—'

A pale hand creaks the door open before I can finish my sentence. My feelings twist and turn in a contradictory nebula of anger, sadness, and compassion.

'Rachel... Jill cared about you a lot,' a gentle voice says. He finally reveals himself, a frail boy with a sickly pale complexion, shimmering diamond eyes, long unkempt dark hair, and puffy red cheeks.

'It was mutual,' I whisper. My emotions now oddly focused and no longer swirling. My resolve solidifies once more.

It is clear. This boy with cheeks red from tears,

with such a gentle nature... He could not have...

'Sorry, but I want to ask you something. Can we talk?'

'Yes, please.' Laurence tilts his head for me to follow him back inside his room. He closes the door behind me, then retrieves a chair from his desk for me and sits on the end of his bed. We sit facing one another. Laurence's eyes nervously dart around the room for an awkward moment before I finally ask him the question that burns in my mind.

'I know you did not kill Jill and I know that it was not just an accident. Please, can you tell me what happened?' I tightly grasp my skirt, holding myself back with anticipation.

Laurence is frozen. His face is a flood of overlapping emotions. Sadness, confusion, happiness, understanding, but not deception. He takes a breath and looks me in the eyes.

'Jill and I used to meet at the balcony for dates. It was a romantic thing. I was out there waiting for her, when I felt a hand tightly grip my shoulder, a black glove. I turned and saw a person draped in shadow, whose features I couldn't quite make out, like something from my subconscious.'

'The Baneful Shade.'

'You know about that? Oh, you probably talked to the guys... I guess that makes sense. Yes, it was the Baneful Shade, but not the one from my head. This one was completely real. I could feel its touch. So I froze, unable to do anything. Then, Jill rushed in and tackled the Baneful Shade. They struggled for only a few seconds, then, the Baneful Shade overpowered Jill and threw her off the balcony. Jill managed to scratch the Baneful Shade's arm and make it bleed, so it ran away as she fell. When I told the police they thought I was crazy and just labelled it as an accident. Sorry

I was useless. I couldn't protect her.' Laurence's eyes hit the floor, tears starting to form at their edges.

I fall into my mind. The world around me disappears and only my thoughts remain.

So the Baneful Shade is real, or rather, it is a person taking on the appearance of the Baneful Shade. If it is a dark shadowy figure, then this person is without a doubt the one who attacked me. In that case, the fake Baneful Shade—the culprit—is someone who had to have been aware of the Baneful Shade before that night. In that case... Wait! Hold on... Could it be her? She knew about the Baneful Shade. It stands to reason from Jill's interactions with her that she knew about the meeting spot and she would have undoubtedly had the opportunity to attack me in the empty halls... But, is there anything definite? Oh, of course! Her arm! At the time, I accepted the lie she told me as a joke, but that is undoubtedly a key clue. That is where the proof is! I am an idiot for not seeing that before. It has all come together. There is no doubt in my mind. She is the culprit.

'Um, are you okay?' Laurence asks, peering into me as I hunch over in deep thought.

Thankfully, I am done with my thoughts. The culprit is clear. I feel immense gratitude I must express. However, before I can, I notice Laurence's sorrowful face. Without thinking, I place my hand on his shoulder. The words that come out of me are not thought out. They clumsily spill from my soul.

'Laurence, I believe you. You did nothing wrong. Jill would never blame you. She would be sad to see you like this. Do not let yourself wallow. Thanks to you I have figured out who killed Jill. Thanks to you I can serve out justice for Jill.' I can feel a half smile on my lips.

'Thank you. I... I don't know what to say...' Laurence sobs.

'You do not have to say anything.' I pat his shoulder, but my mind is elsewhere. My phone buzzes, interrupting my thoughts.

'Um, you can answer,' Laurence says. I feel awkward either way, so I opt to answer the phone.

'Hello. This is Miss Humzy,' the sweet-sounding voice on the other end singsongs.

'Hello, what can I do for you?' I ask, my words somehow come out smoothly, despite the pounding of my heart that echoes and beats like a bongo in my ears.

'Well, tomorrow morning I am holding a group session for Jill's friends. Would you be interested?' This is perfect, in fact, I could not have envisioned a more perfect scenario.

'Hold on, let me put you on speaker. I am with Laurence. He might be interested.' I take the phone away from my ear, press the speaker button and outstretch the phone to Laurence.

'Hello? Laurence? I was wondering if both of you would like to attend a group session about Jill. Her other friends will be there,' Miss Humzy says.

'Yes, I think it would be good for us all to discuss Jill. Right, Laurence?' I wink as I speak. He nods, having seemingly gotten my hint.

'Y-yes,' is his simple yet effective reply.

'Excellent, then I'll see you two tomorrow morning.'

'That you will,' I say.

I hang up the phone. Laurence tilts his head at me. I smile.

'Laurence, tomorrow morning I will enact a plan to catch and arrest Jill's killer. That group session will be the key in that. You do not have to come, but I think you should see justice enacted. I am selfishly doing whatever it takes to find the truth I want, so you should do what you want as well,' I say, excitement welling within me.

'I want to see justice,' Laurence says, exuding conviction far beyond what I expected from him.

'I will see you tomorrow morning then. Thank you, for everything.'

'No, thank you for believing in me and for not giving up on Jill,' he says gratefully, taking me off guard.

'I could not let it go. I was just a bit selfish. That is it, really.'

'That's not a bad thing.' Laurence shows me a smile for the first time. It is so immensely bright I cannot believe it is coming from the same boy as before. I smile as well.

'I suppose not.'

Gathering

Together they form
Truth and lies shamelessly bind
I must see the truth

Chapter 8: The Wisdom of the Long-Suffering Friend

Right now, I'm playing a game and slouching in my room so I can relax. But, it's not working at all. I sigh. I just can't help but worry about Miss Prez.

At lunch she told me that she found Laurence's address through the school register and that she's going to visit him. She told me there's no problem, since she's certain he's not a killer. I don't know where she got that idea, but I guess it makes some sense. Laurence is apparently literally incapable of killing a fly, so I think she's right he's not a murderer. Although, I'm worried about the figure in black who attacked her. Her going alone puts her in an easy position to be attacked, which I don't like at all. Miss Prez told me she would be fine, since if her attacker wanted to kill her, she would already be dead. I'm still not convinced, I mean, it's never a good idea to try and make sense of what's going on in the heads of evil people. But she just asked me to leave it be.

'This has to be very gentle. I need to do this alone.' There it was, Miss Prez being nice, but also somehow demanding. It's annoying as all hell, but I can't help but give in to her. Her demanding but dedicated nature has grown on me. I sigh as I put the controller down, my thoughts going back to the first time I met Miss Prez.

To me, school was always pretty worthless. You

just go do some pointless work, get judged and then be given a score that determines how your life will turn out. I hated it. It really disgusted me. I would always skip class and relax on the grass or lean back in the empty halls instead. There I was, one sunny afternoon, lying on the deserted, peaceful grass.

'Hey, you,' a firm voice said over me. I opened my eyes to see a red-haired girl with sharp green eyes watching me with her hands on her hips, in what was a very clear sign of scolding to come.

'Oh, hey, want to join me? The grass is nice in the warm sun,' I replied as laid back as I possibly could. I thought that would really piss her off.

'No, I would like you to get to class,' she replied without any irritation, kind of like a teacher, but weirdly way more level-headed.

'No thank you. Now if you excuse me, I have some relaxing to get back to.' I yawned and closed my eyes.

'I cannot force you back to class, especially since I have to track down five more class cutters in this study block. However, I will make sure I get to you,' she said before walking off.

'What the hell?' I said aloud, not sure what to make of what had just happened. I was even less sure of what to make of the girl.

I soon discovered what she meant. She was about to shadow me during all of her free blocks. She would always lecture me.

'An education is important. Why are you wasting it?'

'I'm trying to eat lunch here. Can't you leave me alone?'

'No, if you are going to waste your education so readily, I am going to waste your wasted time.'

'Seriously? You're such a pain, Miss Prez.'

'Do not call me that. My name is Rachel.'

'I will if you leave me alone.'

'Then I suppose I will put up with it.'

'Another impasse. Hurray.'

That's how most of our interactions would go, mostly sarcastic or snarky verbal sparring. At first, it truly pissed me off. I thought Miss Prez was a pain in my arse. But after a while, she grew on me. I started to enjoy our little back and forth banter. It was weirdly comforting. At first, I wasn't sure why. Then, one day, it became clear.

'Alright, I'll stop cutting class if you promise to help out. Give me pointers and help me with homework please, Miss Prez,' I said half-jokingly, expecting her to give me a snarky response about how I should do my own homework.

'Of course. I will help you to the best of my ability,' she said without hesitation. It took me off guard. It was then I realised why I found our little sparring matches comforting. Most people in my life who lectured me had no intention of helping me and didn't actually care. They were just doing it because they had to. Miss Prez did want to help me. She truly wanted me to do well. She cared. I couldn't help but smile. It was cheesy and stupid but I didn't care. It was nice.

'Thanks.'

'No problem.' She smiled at me for the very first time, showing a pleasant and welcoming side I never thought I'd see.

My phone buzzes. I tear myself back to the present and swiftly pick up. It's Miss Prez.

'Yo, how did it go?' I ask casually, trying to hide the anxiousness in my voice.

'Excellent! I know who the culprit is beyond a shadow of a doubt.'

'For real?'

'Yes, however, I am going to need your help.'

'My help? What are you planning?' I don't like the

sound of this.

'The groundwork has already been laid. Tomorrow I intend to confront the culprit and make them confess.'

'What? That's way too dangerous. You can't be serious.'

'I am deadly serious, so—'

'No! I can't let you go through with this. I'm not going to let you get yourself killed for some lofty sense of justice. Listen, let's talk to the police and—'

'Do you think the police will do anything without solid evidence? Think about it. We are teenagers with nothing but our words. So, I intend to get irrefutable evidence. But you are mistaken if you think I am doing this for the sake of justice. Lucien, I just want to find the answer for myself. That's it. I'm being selfish. That is all there is to it. So, please listen and help me.' Miss Prez's request takes me off guard.

Just when I think I've caught up to her, she takes a loop around me. This is an incredibly dangerous and stupid idea. Despite that, I simply have to help her. Especially since she's showing off that stubborn and well-meaning selfishness again.

'Alright, I give up. Let's hear your master plan, Miss Prez.'

I'm an idiot, but I guess that's my fault for getting attached to her. Geez, how does she make selfishness so endearing?

Finale

One last move to make
Instants away from the end
Finally, the truth

Chapter 9: The Account of an Ordinary Boy Part 2

We wait in Miss Humzy's office. Michelle taps her foot next to me. I take a deep breath, calming myself and keeping back my worries. I look outside the door, the girl with the hazel bangs from the courtyard looks in and then runs off.

'I can't see a demon! It's that woman! We have to hurry!' she shouts into the phone pressed against her ear as she runs off, it appears that even her fantasies have urgency to them. I don't know if that makes me feel better or stresses me out even more.

'Is everything alright?' Miss Humzy asks with a gentle smile.

'Yeah, I'm just... I guess I'm just a little... I don't know...' I manage.

'That's quite alright. It's only natural you be a little nervous and uncertain. But it's okay, we'll take care of it. Thank you for bringing this to me. It's very brave of you.'

'Thanks, but I just—'

'She's right you know. You're doing good. Not many people would go out of their way for a stranger,' Michelle says.

'You too, Michelle. You're quite nice.'

'How sweet. You know how to make a girl swoon,'

Michelle says with a grin, fanning herself with a hand.

'N-no, I just, I mean, I... Um, I uh—'

'Sorry, sorry, I was just joking,' Michelle chuckles. I let out a relieved breath and my body relaxes but I purse my lips.

Why am I doing this? Why can't I turn away? Who am I?

I don't have the time to answer these questions, since the door to Miss Humzy's office swings open. Rachel and a boy—who I'm guessing is Laurence—walk into the room.

'Oh, Michelle... and Paul?' Rachel stares at me.

'Yes, these two were concerned about you. So, they had me set this up so we could help you,' Miss Humzy explains.

'I see... Thank you. It is due to this gathering I can now expose Jill's killer. Feel free to stay and observe. You have both certainly earned it.' Rachel smirks, her words leave me silent. They sound like nothing you would ever hear in reality, like the sort of thing you would hear in a detective film.

What the hell?

'Rachel, this isn't healthy. What you need is—'

'I am certain Jill was murdered. I can prove it right here and now,' Rachel says firmly.

'Alright then, if you have to. Go for it,' Miss Humzy concedes with a shrug.

'The witness, right here—' Rachel nods to Laurence. '—claims a shadowy figure attacked him. Jill intervened and the figure threw her off the balcony. The police thought this was simply Laurence's imagination, since the shadowy figure resembled a reoccurring hallucination of his. However, two concrete facts prove this figure is undoubtedly real. The first is the blood and skin found underneath Jill's fingernails. Laurence had no scratches anywhere on his body, which must mean Jill scratched the culprit during their struggle. The second point is that the same culprit attacked me in these very halls yesterday morning. This is an irrefutable fact since another person clearly saw the culprit.' Rachel turns to me.

'You mean me?' I ask, bewildered.

'Absolutely. Because you also saw them, you proved that they were real, which in turn helped me deduce the culprit. Thank you.'

Her words evoke both pride and confusion in me, making me wonder if seeing the figure was fate or just a lucky accident.

'Now, since the culprit is real, all that remains is to prove without a doubt who the culprit is. For that, it is clear the culprit had to have known about Laurence's "Baneful Shade" to pull off the killing. The culprit also had to know quite a bit about me, considering they attacked me at an optimal time when I was completely alone. However, the decisive clue is that the culprit has marks from scratches on their body. So, with that the culprit is undoubtedly...' Rachel pauses as she lifts her arm and points. My eyes follow her accusing finger and I am left in silence.

'You! You are the culprit, Karen Humzy!' Rachel proclaims with utter confidence.

'Me? Calm down, Rachel. You—'

'I am calm, calm enough to go through the facts that clearly prove you are the culprit. The first is that because you gave counselling to Laurence, you were familiar with the Baneful Shade. Second, Jill had weekly sessions with you, which would mean you would know a fair amount about her. Building upon that, when you attacked me, you used a recording of Jill's laughter to make me think I was being attacked by a vengeful spirit. Now, that clearly points to you being the culprit. After all, counsellors and psychologists often record their sessions for future reference. However, the decisive clue is the scratches. At first time, I did not think much of the bandages on your arms. I foolishly believed your lie at face value. However, I see now that those were covering up Jill's scratch marks. Thus, you are undoubtedly the killer!'

The room falls silent. No one is sure how to respond. Then, Miss Humzy sighs, and as she does, the air around her completely shifts, warping into something dark and thick. I feel a cold chill up my spine. My body tenses harder than it ever has before. Miss Humzy is completely different from the person we've been in the room with this whole time. My breathing becomes rapid. I've never been so afraid.

'Well done. I certainly underestimated you. I thought you were a brat hiding behind platitudes to protect herself from pain, I expected to see a truth filled with a shallow need for love, but when I attacked you, you showed a far different truth. You showed me such a beautiful truth, one that even bleeds into your life. So, I simply wanted to see that truth grow, I could not bear to pluck it away. I am glad I didn't. Thank you for showing me your beautiful truth in full bloom. You surpassed even my wildest imagination. Yes, I am the culprit you so skilfully found.' Miss Humzy's words make me freeze. Michelle stands up abruptly and backs away from Miss Humzy.

What the hell? What's going on? What is with her?

'You killed Jill? But why? She trusted you! I trusted you. You were so nice. So why? Why?' Laurence screams in a mess of tears.

'That's rather simple. Human beings are liars. My father used to tell my mother "I love you" all the time but would cheat on her without thinking twice. I wanted to find the truth behind people's lies, so I became a counsellor, to see through the lies my clients spit out. I thought I understood human beings, I thought I had grasped the truth at last. Then my father died in front of me, the man who had praised me and showed me love, cursed me as he writhed in his final moments. He showed me naught but spite. He called me a mistake. It was then I realised that I knew nothing at all, that lies will always persist throughout life. However, I also realised the way to truth. My father had shown me his truth in death at last, so all I needed to do to see the truth of others was to view their deaths. Yes, death is the mechanism of truth. It cuts through all lies and displays the truth without fail. You were to be my second window, Laurence, but Jill showed her truth to me instead. You should be happy. Jill truly meant all those words she spoke to you. Her truth shone so brightly,' Miss Humzy says, eyes glazed over.

'You freak!' Michelle spits.

'Monster!' Laurence sobs.

My hands ball into fists. Anger surges through my whole body. I never met Jill. I barely know any of these people. Despite that, I know I hate Miss Humzy from the deepest part of my heart.

'Do not worry. She has just given the proof needed for her arrest to us and the whole internet. You are going to pay for your crimes, Humzy!' Rachel shouts from the depths of herself.

'Oh, is your friend live-streaming this? Clever. The police are already on their way, right? Actually, knowing you, they're probably in the building already. You and that Lucien boy would have planned this extensively. However, you made one miscalculation,' Humzy says as she pulls a pistol from a deep pocket of her jacket. She points it at Rachel.

Damn! I was useless. I wanted to help but I messed up. I did all this to make sure Rachel wasn't hurt again, but I just put her in danger.

'It was hard to acquire, but worth it. Now, the cops watching online can hear me, right? If you don't want Rachel to die, don't get in my way. I'll be taking her with me in my car. I can't stop now. I have to see more of the truth. I need to see the truth of all humans. Don't worry, I'll release her and then be on my way, unless anyone chases after us. Do that and she'll be a corpse,' Miss Humzy says with icy determination as she walks toward Rachel.

I can't let this happen. I can't let her hurt Rachel, or anyone else. Right here and now, I have to stop her.

As these thoughts echo in my mind, I recall how I moved to stop the dark figure, even before I saw Rachel, how I wanted to save her from becoming a victim.

I... I just...

I spring up and tackle Miss Humzy to the floor. A loud bang bursts through the air. I pause. My heart stops and my breathing comes to a halt. I feel fear and dread in all of my being. I can't bring myself to look down.

I don't want to die. I... I... No. With my last seconds of life, I need to save them.

I grit my teeth as tears fall down my face. I look down with all my might. The sight I see makes everything stop. Blood seeps into the carpet, oozing from a hole in Miss Humzy's stomach.

I'm still fine... I'm alive! But she... She...

My mind is empty as I breathe outward. I wheeze. Miss Humzy's cold wet hand touches my cheek. I look down at her again. Miss Humzy's eyes are full of tears. Her breath is short and raspy.

'This is your truth? How... wonderful... But I'm not done yet... I can't die yet... I still need to see... the...

truth... I... have to...' Miss Humzy whispers. Her limp hand falls to the floor.

Blood trickles down my face. My eyes are stuck to the bloody carpet. The image of this moment carves itself into my mind. The final despair of Humzy, set forever in the cold press of death.

Final Chapter: The Abnormal Normality

It's only been two months since the incident with Miss Humzy, yet already, it is fading from the thoughts of some of my peers. They return to their ordinary lives, smiles on their faces and trivial worries within their minds.

I cannot understand. All I have been able to think about is the incident. I have thought about how the police found Miss Humzy's diary filled with haiku, recounting Miss Humzy's distorted recollections of killing Jill and attacking me, and describing her obsession with truth and her 'mechanism'.

I know that my need for truth stemmed from an entirely different place and I know that I would never kill for it. However, it is a frightening parallel between us, that I also became driven to seek the truth for my own selfish want, that I pursued it so recklessly. It honestly makes me horrified.

Am I like her? No, probably not. However, it is undoubtable our searches for truth were both destructive. She was willing to kill and hurt others for her mechanism, and I... I put my truth first. I stupidly and selfishly put it above safety and logic!

I have thought about how in my selfishness I concocted a plan with a major miscalculation, one that could have let Miss Humzy get away and hurt more people. I should have just spoken with the police. Instead, my selfishness would have resulted in a much more dangerous situation, had it not been for Paul.

He stepped up and saved us. I thanked him profusely afterward, but he shook his head and said it was all he could do. I cannot say exactly what he is feeling or thinking, but he seems to be feeling regret.

It is all because of me. Because of me he was put in danger. Because of me he had to see a dead body. Michelle and Laurence too. I put them all in danger and scared them. The worst part is, Miss Humzy's death does not bother me, not in the slightest.

'Stop that.' Lucien's voice sighs from my right.

'Just what do you want me to stop?' I say.

'You're mulling over it all again. Just go back to being the annoying Miss Prez who goes around not minding her own business.'

'It is not that easy.'

'Sure it is. Just stop trying to think about what you could have done.'

'But I—'

'Wait for me to finish, geez. I'm not saying you should forget what you have done. I'm just saying, rather than mulling over what you could have done, you should focus on what you can do now. That's all we really can do.' Lucien smiles. I start to relax.

'That does make sense.'

'Right? Besides, I don't think Paul or Michelle blame you. I talked to them just now. Michelle seemed grateful and Paul... Well, he was doing the same thing you are now. He's been pissed at himself for being "weak". I was going to give him the same spiel I just gave you, but Michelle told him "Keep going. I'll help". That seemed to work and he got his head out of his arse.'

'I see,' I nearly whisper. Pride, guilt, sadness, happiness, worry and contentment, all swirl within me.

However, I stop indulging in my emotions before they can overwhelm me.

If they're moving forward, so will I. I have to. I cannot leave myself to wallow in self-pity while everyone else is doing something worth a damn.

'Thank you, Lucien. That helped. I will keep on going. I will do whatever I can,' I resolutely proclaim.

'That's what I like to hear. Sounds like Miss Prez is back in her full glory. Oh right, don't you have somewhere to be soon?'

'Crap!' I had nearly forgotten. I bolt up and run. I hear Lucien laugh.

'How can you be so reliable, yet also such a dolt?'

'Shut up!' Despite my words, a smile is on my lips.

Laurence stands beside me. We are the only ones in this desolate place. We stare at Jill's grave, the headstone one of many in four neat rows. Silence fills the air.

The two of us have so many thoughts, so many feelings going through our minds. We do not need to voice them aloud. Just being here and being able to reflect upon her together is enough. In fact, it is quite refreshing. A piece of remembrance. It quells my overthinking mind. So, we enjoy the shared silence. Eventually though, it ends.

'Thank you, for believing me, for finding Jill justice,' Laurence whispers.

'To be honest, when I started investigating, I thought you did it, and my reasons for doing it were nothing noble like getting justice.'

'There's nothing wrong with doing something right for the wrong reasons. It's okay to be selfish sometimes.' Laurence's words make me chuckle.

'Jill said something similar to me once. I can see where she got it from now.'

'Did she? When I told her those same words, she said I was "too cute" and just laughed.'

'She was always like that. She would laugh things off but then seriously keep them in mind.'

'Yeah, she was a bit of a contradiction at times. But that's why I loved her.' Laurence smiles. I follow suit.

'Yes, it was hard not to treasure her.' I feel tears running down my cheeks.

Thank you, Jill, for so much in my life. I will do what I can in the here and now. I will not hesitate or procrastinate. Thank you, please watch over us, alright?

Epilogue: A Lazy Day

'So, it handled itself? That's convenient for us.' I shrug.

'Why are you always so lazy? I know most demon extermination missions are pretty boring and easy, especially given your power, but I wish you would be less laid back. Besides, I was the one who had to do all the actual infiltration. Do you know how embarrassing it is to wear a high school uniform at my age, Saki?' My husband huffs as he folds his arms. I can't help but chuckle as I grasp his tiny frame and sit him on my lap. 'H-hey, don't patronise me,' he says as I stroke his soft hazel hair.

'Oh, come on, Kit. You look adorable in a skirt. I mean, you never complain when I ask you to wear a sailor uniform,' I say as I play with his silky strands of hair.

'That's different. You're my wife. Doing it in front of other people is embarrassing, especially kids.'

'But you're way too pretty. It'd be suspicious to have you dress as a boy.'

'You just want to take pictures of me in a skirt.'

'No way, I burned the image into my mind's eye.'

'Moron.'

'You know, you're adorable when you're annoyed. I should annoy you more often.'

'Don't!' He shouts. His pleading eyes are way too cute to deny.

'I was just kidding,' I say with a laugh.

I do want to see his pouting face more though...

'A-anyway, that Rachel girl was certainly impressive, wasn't she? We were sent in because the Order detected negative energy at the scene of Jill Helter's murder. Yet, that girl figured out the culprit and almost bested her without any techniques or spiritual awareness.'

'Yeah, I was just going to leave it to her. She figured it all out before us. But even we didn't expect Humzy would pull a gun. Good thing I used my Absolute God Hand technique to redirect that gunshot, or it would have killed that poor boy,' I say as I stroke my chin. I recall the look on Rachel's face. She just glared at Humzy and stood her ground, despite the gun in her face.

What kind of person are you, Rachel Walker?

I chuckle.

'What is it?'

'I was just thinking I'd like to meet that Rachel Walker one day.'

'For an ordinary person, she is quite striking. Maybe next time you could infiltrate the school and talk with her.'

'No way, I'm way too tall and cool to be a believable student.'

'Moron. Just be a teacher.'

'No way, a free spirit like me can't be a stupid pencil pusher.'

'You are a complete moron, are you aware of that?'

'Yep, I'm aware. That's why I'm so loveable.'

'You're not wrong,' Kit whispers, his face turned away so I can't see the blush that is most certainly there.

How cute.

'Your bluntness is why I love you,' I tease him as I stroke his hair.

'Back to the report, what technique did Ellie Hancock use?' A woman's voice cuts in.

An interloper. A rude one at that. I have to punish them!

I turn to see a woman in an obnoxiously frilly red dress. Her stupid umbrella blocks the bright beams of light above.

'Faust, I would kill you if it was possible.' I gnash my teeth, trying to glare her away.

Stupid Faust, always putting your nose where it doesn't belong. If there weren't rules against it—No, to hell with those rules. I'd kill you a thousand times if it weren't for your stupid immortality.

'Don't be rude, Saki. I apologise, Fraulein Faust. What a pleasure to see you,' Kit replies politely. I can feel his glare on me even as I death-stare Faust.

He's so cute even when he's pissed off, but why does he have to be polite with her?

'Hello, Kit. I just wish your wife would be more friendly. It's been ten years, can we not bury the hatchet?' Faust asks as she extends her hand to me.

'Of course not. You could have stopped Kujo from leaving the Order, but you let him go and my best pal in the world was hurt really bad. I'll never forgive you, you selfish bitch.'

'Sorry, but Kujo is my "best pal in the world." I could only respect his decision to leave. Besides, how was I to know his plans?'

'How convenient.'

'A-anyway, Fraulein Faust, you asked about Humzy's, or rather, Hancock's, technique, right?' Kit stammers.

'Yes, I am curious to know what it actually did. If she could not fight off an ordinary person, she must have been quite weak.'

'You are correct. Her technique is called Fear In The Dark. It simply projects the fears of a target into reality, using the technique as a medium. That made us think that there was a demon, we assumed that Laurence's statement to the police was him seeing a demon. In my investigation, I was seeking the trail of a demon's negative energy. However, when I considered that it might not be a demon, I did some research and found Hancock in the records. From there, I simply searched for her negative energy, until I found a slither emanating from that so-called Ms Humzy. Though, I only managed to do so when she had a room of students in her clutches, thankfully Saki was in time to save them,' Kit explains.

He's so cute when he's smart.

'I see. It was merely an illusion technique. I suppose it somewhat fits as the power of a delusional murderer.' Faust twirls her golden hair as she ponders her own words.

It's not profound or anything. Just piss off already.

'Although, that Rachel Walker girl is certainly interesting. I mean, she fixed a problem with such prowess that stumped Kit the Limitless Shadow and the Divine Paladin Saki Sato. Consider this, Humzy so easily hid her negative energy and her technique so proficiently that she almost got away with it; especially given her plastic surgery. Yet, a schoolgirl with no powers managed to reveal Humzy. Even after all these years, people never cease to amaze me. She reminds me of another promising person I happened to come across a while back,' Faust muses as her damn blue eyes look past us.

'Who would that be, old hag?'

I hate to admit it, but she's got me curious. Another incredible person like Rachel Walker being out there gets me excited.

'Her name is Kyoko Nakamura. I recommend you remember it,' Faust replies with a smirk.

'The first-born Nakamura child with no technique or negative energy? That one?' Kit asks.

'The very same. You two have already observed power beyond techniques or energy. I would say Kyoko is a person who has a power far more incredible than any technique. I shall leave you with that. A lady must always maintain an air of mystique and leave just as things get interesting. Although, do not think I didn't hear you calling me an "old hag" Saki,' Faust says as she turns and walks away.

'I wanted you to hear it, dumbarse!' I curse at her as I raise my fist.

'Must you always get so easily riled up? Honestly, you are not a child,' Kit says through a deep sigh.

'Ah, sorry... So, Kyoko Nakamura, huh? I'll look forward to meeting her,' I say as a smile finds its way to my lips.

Yeah, people like that, they're the ones who'll change this world. I'll lend them my power and help them get rid of the fossils that prevent change. That's right, Faust. I will remember Kyoko Nakamura and I'll help her to rid this world of you.

EXORCIST DANCE: VERSE OF THE REVOLUTION

Chapter 0: Death+Truth

On the 5th of April 2035, Toji Kujo opened a passage to the world of the Administrator. Caroline Cooper sealed the passage away with a powerful technique that cannot be dispelled, but the technique had a time limit of five months.

Kujo spent those five months gathering powerful allies from the underworld and the forgotten victims of the Exorcist world. To do so, he made a pact with the Demon King Letrith, the matriarch of supreme thunder by unsealing her. In exchange, she began a rampage across the African continent. The sheer power and damage from Letrith forced the Exorcist Order to send all of their available Exorcists and four of the six Paladins to combat the threat. This left Kujo free to act, with only Caroline and the nine young Exorcists-in-training, those exempt from normal duty, from her special class able to oppose Kujo.

To prepare for the battle, they spent five months training to become stronger and overcome Kujo. Most notably, Julie Vance and Kyoko Nakamura submitted to brutal training under Caroline. Julie trained to be strong enough to resist being taken over by the angel inside her, Lucifer the Angel of Knowledge, and to gain access to Lucifer's spatial technique freely in battle. Kyoko trained to hone her body and mind to such a level that she could destroy all enemies in her way.

On the 5th of September 2035, the seal was about

to open. Kujo and his allies waited in the city. Caroline prepared to face her old master as students moved in to stop him before midnight, the hour when the portal to The Room of Creation would open.

Excerpt from *The Birth of the World*, by Comos Snow, 1981

The Room of Creation is the place where the world is managed and overlooked by the Administrator. The Administrator of our world is The Messiah who, two thousand years ago, killed the old gods of myth and legend and usurped their title of Administrators. He shaped the world as it is and currently overlooks it. The specifics of his power are unknown, however, it is known that he is confined to The Room of Creation. This is known because of the knowledge Fraulein Faust granted humanity. In essence, The Room of Creation confines the Administrator, or Administrators, to govern only within the room, unable to leave it for the rest of their existence in that role. This is why the old gods used angels as their representatives in this world. Furthermore, the only way an Administrator can leave is to relinquish their form, memories, and power to reincarnate as a human. The Room of Creation cannot be left by an Administrator, but The Room of Creation can be entered by a human. Fraulein Faust claims the current Administrator was only able to gain access because of Himiko, the only Exorcist in history who had the ability to create entirely new, but temporary, doors to other dimensions. The only other way to gain access to The Room of Creation is to force the door open by creating a portal into The Room of Creation. Currently, no such method for this exists. To do that is to challenge the Administrator's world, an act foretold to begin an apocalypse called the Day of Destruction. The usurper who opens the door would face the Administrator and have one day to defeat him. If they were to fail, the current Administrator's world would be maintained. If they were to win, they would become the new Administrator and the only damage would be the complete destruction of land and life directly surrounding the portal. However, if the usurper wins, but the time limit is passed, the current world would be entirely destroyed. The usurper would then become the new Administrator, able to create a new world of their own design.

Chapter 1: Vs Kujo's Followers/The Potential of the Future

05/09/2035 9:00 PM

Moonlight enveloped the city. An unnerving quiet encroached upon the five men in suits who stood in the empty streets. The desolate sidewalks, depilated buildings, and soft evening wind presented an eeriness that did not fit a city that had once bustled with life. Each man felt the cool breeze distinctly touch his soul. However, they did not consider leaving, nor did they voice their grievances aloud, for they served a master, to which they owed everything. So, there they waited. They were ready to dispatch his enemies at a moment's notice.

'There! An enemy!' the suited man with a scar over his left eye called out as he raised his assault rifle at the figure before him. The man's four other companions quickly raised their assault rifles to place a bead on the figure, a teenage girl.

Her dark track jacket blended into the night as it gripped her body. Her sneakers soundlessly pressed forward, step by silent step. The sheathed blade that hung at the girl's waist told the men who she was. Their master had told them of all the Exorcists they would face tonight, the young woman with the Black Blade was the one they should be most cautious of. These men of unerring loyalty did not hesitate for an instant before they fired upon Kyoko Nakamura. Kyoko did not hesitate either.

With inhuman speed and agility, Kyoko rushed forward. As though in a dance, her body gracefully flowed between the bullets. She swiftly reached the first man, smashed her hilt into his throat and slammed him into unconsciousness. The next men were swift to follow. Kyoko's right knee crashed into the second's face while her left elbow bore into the third man's cheek. The fourth man abandoned his rifle. He drew a switchblade from his back pocket and charged. Kyoko effortlessly caught his assailing arm, snapped it, threw him to the ground and gave a powerful kick that rendered him immobile. The fifth man took this opportunity and fired while Kyoko's back was turned to him. Kyoko released her sword from its scabbard with a hiss of steel. With a single neat stroke, the bullets were sliced in half and fell to the ground with a pitter-patter as though they were mere raindrops, turned aside by an umbrella. In the next instant, Kyoko's blade tore through the man's neck. His body slumped to the ground. Kyoko flicked the blood off her Black Blade and softly slid it back within its sheath.

'Sorry, I was trying to hold back from killing, but you got too far in my way... Though... I have gotten stronger. Maybe this time I can protect them...' Kyoko's fist tightened as her eyes darted toward the pool of the man's blood. Her heart pounded as her lip began to tighten. Her mind drifted back to the first time she had ended a human life, toward Yelena.

I see, you truly do not get used to it... Good... But... No, I won't hesitate.

'I will protect them, no matter what I have to do,

no matter how many enemies I have to cut down.' Kyoko's eyes drifted upward. She gazed toward the moon. Its light brushed away the pounding of her heart.

'We only have three hours until Master Caroline's barrier breaks down. I need to hurry.' Kyoko turned to the city, to the centre of the concrete jungle.

'Kujo, I won't let you have your way this time!' Kyoko proclaimed as she broke into a run.

05/09/2035 9:05 PM

'She took out that entire squad by herself, not that I expected anything different but...' Kujo whistled.

'What is it, Master?' asked a short girl with frizzy chestnut hair and a white hoodie, leaning in toward Kujo.

'It is nothing, Fei, or nothing particularly bad. Kyoko Nakamura has grown tremendously over these short five months, so much so that even I am in awe,' Kujo said, a sheepish chuckle escaped his lips.

I assumed Caroline was bluffing. She was always particularly good at bluffing when we played Mah-jong. Yet... the reality is too clear. Although, I suppose I knew that already. After all, Caroline, I was also preparing these last five months. Your technique will release in three mere hours. When it does, this world will change forever. I will use everything I have to ensure the barrier opens, and this world finally changes.

'Yeah, but even so, you can beat her with ease, Master! Not that it will come to that. She'll be dead before she reaches you!' Fei beamed, taking Kujo from his thoughts and bringing a quiet smile to his face.

'I appreciate the thought, but it is not good to underestimate your opponent, especially one like this.'

'Which is why you hired me, right?' Kujo and Fei turned to the voice. A woman with ash blond hair yawned. Her right hand sat within the pocket of her dark denim jeans, while a plain Romanesque short sword rested on her left hip.

'Precisely, June. There is a reason you are called the Untouchable Exorcist after all,' Kujo chuckled.

'Is that really what people call me? That's lame. It's even worse than "The Null Woman." Why are my peers and enemies so shoddy at nicknames?' June let out a long sigh, ruffling her plain white t-shirt.

'Anyway, what are your orders, Master?' Fei said, throwing a glare at June. June turned away from her and yawned again.

'Fei, mobilise the twins and head out. Make sure nobody gets here just yet. Well, except for Caroline. You won't be able to beat her and I want to settle the score with her myself. June, go and hunt down Kyoko Nakamura. If you find any others, feel free to eliminate them. You will be compensated for each additional Exorcist you eliminate. However, your main priority is killing Kyoko Nakamura above all else,' Kujo commanded. Fei nodded fervently and rushed off. June peered at Kujo.

'Are you sure you want me to concentrate on killing just one girl? Is she really that strong?'

'She is strong. Not strong enough to threaten me, but she has grown rapidly. I fear she must be taken out before her fangs grow enough to put me at risk. Although... honestly, she reminds me of a man I met long ago, a man who was the strongest I ever knew. Her presence now feels so much like his. It is unnerving.'

'The strongest? Are you telling me he was stronger than Saki Sato?'

'If they fought, it would be close, but the adaptability of Saki Sato's Absolute God Hand technique would lead her to prevail. In fact, she could possibly even defeat Lucifer.'

'So he's not as strong as that monstrous woman. That's a relief. Then, was he stronger than you?

'Yes, by far.'

'Damn, you've given me a hell of a gig. Though, as long as I don't have to fight Saki Sato ever again, I'm fine. You're paying me well and Kyoko Nakamura is still just a kid. This should be simple. I just hope that girl won't be too much of a pain in the arse... I'll be expecting a bonus when I bring you her corpse.' June gave a lethargic wave as she walked off.

Kujo looked at the stars. 'Kyoko is frighteningly like you, Akihiko. Were you alive, you would no doubt find my methods despicable. Sorry, old friend, but I cannot turn away now. I must change the world. I must destroy the Administrator and his decrepit world. I must bring forth change at all costs.'

Gears

Tick, tick, tick
Carefully laid out,
Like seeds in a field
They now come together
Together,
The world will be changed
as they sprout toward the heavens

Excerpt from *The Blades of Sukeroku I* **by Sukeroku III, 1958**

My grandfather created one hundred great blades throughout his life. At present, sixty of them are used by Exorcists, four are looked after by my son, two are looked after by my daughter, five are looked after by myself, seven are sealed away, nine have been destroyed, twelve are kept in reserve in branches across the world and Fraulein Faust carries the last blade. That blade alone is special. Fraulein Faust collaborated with my grandfather to make the ultimate weapon, indestructible and capable of destroying any demon. Fraulein Faust used her technique to form an indestructible black metal and imparted it with the ultimate sword attribute, Pierce, the attribute that gives a sword the ability to pierce souls and kill the undying. My grandfather took this metal and refined it for twelve days. At the end of the twelfth day, The Black Blade, the invincible god-killing sword, was born. My grandfather insisted Fraulein Faust take it with her. Before my grandfather's death in 1932, my father asked him why he gave Fraulein Faust the sword. My grandfather answered that he believed a blade of such power should have a wielder who would use it well, who would not simply wave its great power around and let it go to their head. He asked that Fraulein Faust use her endless life to find such a wielder. Fraulein Faust accepted and took it with her. In fact, she took this role so seriously that only five years later, she campaigned the Order to instate a rule that ensured Exorcist weapons and tools could only be taken from an Exorcist if all Paladins unanimously agreed upon the weapon confiscation, or else be considered a punishable offence. This came into effect four years later in 1910.

Chapter 2: Vs The Horde/A Sad Master

'I'm going to throw a wrench into Kujo's plan from the outside,' Caroline said. 'Yuya, Jacob and Erica, I'm trusting the three of you to keep Kujo busy. Mikoto, stay back and watch. Don't move in unless someone is about to die. Atuy and Veronica, your job is to keep the heat off the others by engaging any strong enemies and keeping their attention on you. Ethan, I trust your judgement, so act as our sniper and support anyone in need. Julie and Kyoko have probably already made it inside. I need you all to believe in them and stick to your jobs. The two of them have become far stronger than I could have imagined five months ago, so please, trust in me—no—in them, and I'll trust in all of you.'

05/09/2035 10:00 PM

Erica, Yuya and Jacob rushed toward Kujo's location, following the directions Caroline had given them. Ten or so men in suits with assault rifles bore down on the group. As Jacob understood it, these were ordinary people Kujo had recruited. However, these people were vagrants, lowly criminals and those otherwise discarded by society. Since Kujo had given these people a place and purpose, it made sense they were willing to kill and die for him. This did not deter Jacob, for he was also resolved to do what it took to stop Kujo's ambition from flourishing.

'Lighting Focus: Magnetic Pull.' Jacob focused on the new application of his technique. He manipulated the negative energy in his palm to transition the lighting form of his energy into a magnetic force that ripped the assault rifles from the grips of his enemies.

'Binding Chain: Earth Ceremony.' Yuya's follow-up swiftly wrapped the men in chains. The ends of the chains separated from Yuya and bound themselves to the ground.

A new man revealed himself with a grenade launcher over his shoulder.

'My turn! Allow me to show you something special. Technique Activation Control: Speed Force!' Erica smirked as she increased the flow of negative energy in her feet. She darted to the man and sent him to the land of nod with a punch that echoed through the quiet night.

'Good job. Our training paid off, but we don't have time to stand around. We have to hurry to Kujo.' Erica cracked her knuckles as she uttered his name. Jacob clicked his tongue. Yuya nodded.

'Is that right? Sorry, missy, you're not going anywhere. Well, not unless you want your friend here to die.' A voice cackled behind Jacob. Before anyone could react, a knife was at his throat, held by a man with a toothy grin. Two other men appeared from the shadows.

'You were expecting us, huh? What a pain. Jacob, Yuya, don't hesitate. Fight them with everything you have. Don't hold back because they're normal humans,' Erica commanded firmly, her gaze settled on the captor.

'Cocky little brat, aren't you? You need to keep quiet or I'll slit his—' The man was unable to finish his sentence. Jacob used the man's knife as a lightning rod to conduct just enough power to instantly knock the man out, without shattering his bones or putting a hole in him.

Yuya flung out a pointed chain that pierced through the heart of the second man. As blood poured from the man's mouth he looked into Yuya's eyes, within which, the man saw a cold resolve as he left the mortal coil.

Erica slammed her fist into the third man and flung him to the ground.

In the silence, Yuya gazed upon his hand.

'I just killed someone...'

'You didn't hesitate to defend a friend, that's all,' Erica spoke quietly.

'But, I could have chosen better. I could have spared him,' Yuya's eyes fell to the ground.

'Maybe you could have, but he was trying to kill us. It was kill or be killed, and you chose the former. It's as simple as that.' Jacob placed his hand on Yuya's shoulder.

'I... Right, I bear these sins for the sake of my friends' lives. Let's head to Kujo.'

'Yes, let's hurry,' Erica said before she bounded off, followed swiftly by a steadfast Yuya and Jacob.

05/09/2035 10:15 PM

'There!' Jacob called out as the group rushed into the

centre of the city. It was an open square with very little within it. Very little except for Kujo, who did not react to Jacob's proclamation. Instead, tears fell from his eyes as he gazed upward at the moon as its crème light shone down upon him.

'Fei, Tina, Tony, everyone... I am sorry. Thank you for giving everything. I will not allow your lives to be wasted. I vow to you all, this world will be changed,' Kujo spoke solemnly, head still tilted to the moon.

Jacob lunged at Kujo. Erica slowed Kujo's flow of negative energy and sped up her own. Yuya hurled a chain at Kujo.

In an instant, Kujo faded into the air itself. Three blows hit the three of them. Disappointment, frustration and apologies flashed through their minds before they hit the ground and fell into a deep slumber. Kujo reappeared and let out a small breath. 'The Null Technique is certainly effective. I am sure June can defeat Kyoko. It truly cannot be stopped when combined with the element of surprise. However... why did I not kill them?' Kujo looked down upon Erica, Jacob and Yuya's unconscious bodies. He continued to speak to the shadows. 'I could have easily cut them down. I did not hesitate to send an assassin after Kyoko Nakamura. So then, why did I hesitate now?'

'I would have thought you know why you hesitated. After all, you're still an idealistic fool, old Master,' a familiar voice laughed behind Kujo.

'Yes, I suppose I still foolishly want these children to see the new world and live happily within it,' Kujo conceded with a chuckle as he turned to the voice.

'Sorry, Kujo, but your world will never come to fruition. My preparations have made certain of that.' Caroline cracked her knuckles as she walked out of a shadow, her presence now no longer hidden within it. She stood face to face with Kujo.

'How troublesome. I suppose I will have to crush this plan of yours. Though, I wish you had joined me in realising this new world.'

'You know there's no way I would ever do that. Besides, I wish you could have just stayed my master.'

'I see. I truly am sorry, my dear student.'

'Me too.'

The cold wind blew through the silence, the calm before the end of their bond.

Wish

Despite it all,
I simply want to turn back
All I wish for,
Is to once more journey with you
To land without sorrow

Excerpt from *The Extensive Guide to Curse Techniques* by A J Spirit, 2029

There are currently three Exorcist families that possess curse techniques: the Williams family from Wales, the Acharya family from India, and the Seidel family from Germany. There were four, but the Curse Reflection technique from China's Lan family has disappeared since their conflict with the Tao family, who possess purification techniques. The Tao were punished and forced to become stewards of the Order, but the Lan and their Curse Reflection technique were lost. Of all the curse-based techniques, Curse Reflection was by far the strongest. After all, unlike the other curse techniques, Curse Reflection could kill an enemy after they inflict any injury, unlike other techniques, which can only deal damage in an equivalent or slightly higher field of damage. Furthermore, it could apparently summon a great dark being that embodied hatred. However, the activation cost and the specifics of this have been lost with the Lan.

Chapter 3: Vs Sniper and Wildcard

Fei had been born unwanted, tossed aside as though she were garbage by those who begrudgingly called themselves her parents.

'You are weak. How pathetic.'

'You don't deserve to live, scum. To think we escaped the Tao, only to find our great family's revival ruined by a weakling like you, scum who can't even control her technique.'

Day after day, she trudged through the seemingly unending hatred around her, until Fei spoke a thought that fizzled into her mind.

'I wish it would all just go away.'

With those words, Fei made corpses of those abhorrent people. They were distorted beyond any notion of human shape whatsoever. Initially, Fei found joy in this. She felt blessed, as though a god had finally heard her prayers and struck those disgusting people down in a horrid way fitting for their horrid existence.

This initial wave of joy did not last long. Fei quickly realised it was not another entity that granted her wish, but herself. She was the one in possession of a horrid, cruel, terrifying power and with it she had truly made herself alone. Surely no one would accept her. This power would only destroy and kill all those around her.

Fei spent a year in isolation with only concrete for her pillow, alone in alleyways, ignored upon the empty streets as she shivered through cold nights.

That was until *he* appeared. With a smile, he extended his hand to her. He pulled Fei to her feet and gave her a place to belong. He showed Fei how to control and use her curse power, how to channel it, how to restrain it and how to use it as she pleased. He did all this and asked for nothing in return. Fei decided she would follow him no matter what. She decided she would become his sword and strike down his enemies. That was her place within this world. Anyone who shared this goal with her was her comrade. Fei felt she understood those people better than anyone else possibly could. Except for June. The thought of her brought a scowl to Fei's face. Fei could not understand how June looked upon their righteous battle with such indifference, how all she believed in were mere pieces of paper. Her teeth gnashed against each other. Her mind boiled at the thought of that woman.

That stupid woman is not worth my time. I need to focus on hunting Master Kujo's enemies. I must maintain a calm mind, so I can kill them without error.

Fei stopped, let out a deep breath and proceeded further into the city.

05/09/2035 10:10 PM

Fei found ten of her comrades dead, with a neat bullet hole in each of their temples. Fei bit her lip and closed her eyes. Just like her, all her comrades had been tossed aside by the world around them. Kujo had given them all a place and had accepted them without conditions. As such, they all shared the same intention and purpose. They all simply wished to repay the kindness Kujo bestowed upon them. Fei could not help but give in to sentiment.

'Don't worry. I won't let them pass. I promise,' Fei whispered before she opened her eyes and focused on her surroundings. It was abundantly clear her comrades had been taken out by a sniper.

It was a skilled sniper at that, one that's probably alone. Cowardly bastard! How dare they pick away my defenceless comrades from a distance. I can't even get close enough to hit him. They'd take me out in one shot. I could avoid dying, survive the first shot, but I'd be made useless. Wait, if I survive, then I can activate my technique... My technique just needs me to get hurt by a person or demon, then I can activate my technique and curse them to death. This means I can win! But, there's no guarantee I'll survive. They could kill me right away and I'll achieve nothing.

Fei gazed down at her comrades' corpses. Heat filled her body.

No, I have to try. All I need to do is survive the first shot and then I can curse them to death.

Fei pursed her lips. It was a risky plan. This sniper was an excellent shot, one that would not be so easily evaded. However, Fei had no fear of death nor of being hurt. Her resolve allowed her to move forward with only the thought of killing the sniper. She rushed forward. Her movements became rapid and erratic in an effort to evade the inevitable shot.

Come on!

Fei turned a corner. She bolted forward in a wild zigzag.

Come on! Come on! Come on!

A loud bang permeated the air. A bullet soared

toward Fei. It crashed into her chest. A small hole opened with a flicker of blood as the bullet dug itself into Fei's torso, resting deep in her diaphragm. Fei fell to the ground, her blood pooled onto the concrete and created a sickening warmth as she lay there.

'Curse Reflection: Death Strikes!' Fei said through a gasp of air. She clicked her fingers.

Silence followed. Fei did not hear, see or feel anything that gave her purchase. She did not need to, for her technique had never failed to kill an enemy who had harmed her. Fei felt confident she had managed to kill one of her master's enemies.

She forced herself to her feet through a wince. Almost immediately, her body's energy seeped out and it took all Fei had to remain on her feet.

Just a bit more. I need to keep going for just a little more.

Through a pained breath, Fei took a step forward, only for a familiar figure to appear before her, a petite blonde girl with ocean-blue eyes overflowing with a sea of tears.

'I told Ethan to stay behind. He was still recovering... But he didn't listen. He insisted on being our sniper, our protector from above. I failed to save him and you... You're a murderer now. You're still so young, but you're part of all this fighting and killing,' the girl uttered through thick sobs.

Fei did not register her words in the slightest. All she saw was Julie, the vessel of Lucifer.

No! No, no, no! If she gets past me, she could destroy Master's ambitions!

'I'll bring someone to heal you, so just stay here and think about all this, alright? Think about all the death and destruction, about all the pain,' Julie uttered as she outstretched her hand to Fei.

'No! I won't let you get in the way of my master's

plan! Oh, God of Malice, I feed you my life! Destroy my enemy and reduce them to nothing!' Fei screamed. Negative energy poured out of her. Her body grew weak, and her eyelids began to shut.

Master, please understand... I love you... We all do... So please... achieve... your goal...

Fei's eyes glimpsed the beauty of the ever-bright moon before they shut forever. Her negative energy formed a massive humanoid beast covered in a mass of curses, a final hate-filled attack driven by love.

Why?

Why must we kill each other?
Why do we have to fight?
Why did you kill my friend?
Why did you die just to stop me?
Couldn't we talk?
Couldn't we understand one another?
Why is it all so pointless?
Why must everyone die for this stupid fight?
Oh world,
Please answer me!

Excerpt from Livio Raine's 2007 address to the Exorcist Order

I am sure it is common knowledge to everyone here that talented young Exorcists are valued. That is why we need to put more protections and systems in place to protect these children from those who would exploit them. There are so many stories of talented children being stolen from their parents and used as test subjects in projects to create stronger Exorcists. Ladies and gentlemen, surely exploiting these children and turning them into living weapons is something we all agree is worth stopping. To that end, I want us all to work together to protect these children, to rescue those who have already been taken and to shut down all of these research projects. Toji Kujo is already on board. With your help, we can save the children together.

Chapter 4: Vs The Twins

A pair of children appeared before Atuy and Veronica upon a dilapidated balcony fence that precariously craned itself above the city. The two shared the same dark blue eyes and long raven hair. The boy's white and blue striped navy uniform and the girl's long dark dress thrashed in the cool wind. The boy sneered down at Atuy and Veronica, the girl gave a smile darker than night. Veronica hesitated. She considered reaching out to the children before her, but Atuy stood in front of her, his glare pointed squarely toward the children.

'These children do not have any mercy. Do not hold back,' Atuy exhaled as his body tensed. All the muscles in his body were primed to move in a split second.

'Aw, they figured us out already, Tina! Usually the grownups are so dumb.' The boy sighed.

'Yeah, it's so easy when they think we're just poor children, Tony. I guess we'll just have to work harder to kill them.' Tina smiled as her eyes darted to Veronica.

In that instant, Atuy let his guardian spirit attack. Its powerful fist ruptured through the air, slammed into Tina and struck her down onto the concrete floor of the balcony.

'Tina, you should let this bad man feel some pain,' Tony snickered as he grasped his right cheek, a mark grew bright red from a powerful punch.

'Yeah, here's your stupid punch back! Karmic Reflection: Plus Two!' Tina chuckled as she got to her feet. The punch mark was completely gone from her face. Atuy's head slammed backward as blood spilled from his mouth.

'We need to stop attacking. They'll only reflect them back at us!' Veronica cried out.

'Indeed, the brother transfers the damage from his sister to himself, then the sister directs double damage to her opponent. It is annoying, but we will wait.' Atuy's eyes moved toward the brother. Veronica understood what the gesture meant, but she hesitated and sucked in the air harshly.

'Look, look! They're still holding back,' Tony chuckled as he pointed to Atuy.

'Yeah, they're dumb grownups. Those are always the most enjoyable to kill.' Tina laughed as she punched herself in the gut. Tony recoiled at the blow with a grunt, though a smile remained on his lips even as blood cascaded from his mouth and stained a white patch of his uniform red. Atuy coughed blood, struggling to hold himself upright.

'Atuy!' Veronica called out.

'F-focus.' Atuy winced. His composure and eyes had not shifted in the slightest.

'Stupid grownups. Did you really think we wouldn't have a strategy to kill you guys when you stop attacking? This is why killing stupid adults is the most fun thing in the world,' Tony said.

'Yeah, you all say things like "you're just kids" and "I can't kill children." It makes killing so much more enjoyable. You stupid adults hurt us, neglected us, damaged us and excused yourselves by saying we were just test subjects. But now, you can't even lay a hand on us. It's super pathetic.'

'You...' Veronica's voice croaked. She winced as she imagined the suffering of the young children before her. It horrified her. It made her knees weak.

No, they aren't my enemies. They're just kids. I can still—

'Veronica, stop that. Look closer. It is far too late for them. These pitiful souls have bathed in blood and suffering for far too long. They enjoy this world of killing too much. After all, their techniques are well suited to swiftly immobilising an enemy. They could have doubled a strike that would have knocked me out or perhaps even killed me. Yet, I still live. These two want to relish our torture. That is why we must swiftly act,' Atuy said firmly. Veronica's eyes darted to the ground as her lip quivered.

'Wow, for a stupid grown up you actually get it.' Tony beamed.

'What?'

'But you said it like it's a bad thing. It's not! Slowly killing stupid adults, watching them not even try to fight back and seeing how pathetic their last moments are as they try to reach out to us. It's the most enjoyable thing in the entire world,' Tina chuckled.

'Yeah! And you can't take it away from us. It's our right,' Tony chimed in.

They enjoy killing others, people who try to help them, who don't even fight back. These two are... They're corrupted. So I'll save them!

Veronica pointed squarely at Tina.

'You won't suffer anymore, I promise. Land's Healer: Spark Flare.' Veronica released a small ball of flame at Tina. It struck her flesh only to immediately fizzle away and transfer to Tony.

'Nice try, but now you will suffer!' Tony shouted. He wildly tried to swat the flame away from his shoulder. The small flame came back as a soccer ball-sized fireball and hurtled toward Veronica, but floated to a stop before it could hit her.

'My technique gives me complete control of flames. Surrender and I'll deactivate my technique, otherwise, my flames will burn you forever,' Veronica said.

This should do it. They can't win now. They'll have to realise it.

'Damn you, stupid grownup! Tina, hurt yourself and then I'll kill this stupid adult!' Tony roared as the flame seared into his flesh. He fell to his knees as tears rolled down his cheeks.

'Alright, let's make her suffer for thinking she could beat us. We'll just kill her and stop her technique that way!' Tina screamed as she raised a fist, ready to strike herself.

Veronica fired an additional flame at Tina, who reflexively transferred it to Tony. Tony screamed as more flames etched into his body.

'I'll kill you! I'll absolutely kill you! Stupid grownup!' Tony howled. The flames consumed his body, his form only barely visible through the blaze.

'Stop! No!' Veronica cried out. She deactivated her technique. Tony's form slumped to the floor of the balcony. Smoke drifted from the charred remains.

'T-Tony? Tony! Don't leave me! Please, don't leave...' Tina sobbed. Veronica fell to her knees.

'So you're not coming back? Then, I'll come with you, Tony...' Tina pulled a knife from her pocket.

She sliced her throat open.

'No!' Veronica screamed.

Atuy moved his guardian spirit up to the balcony. Tina's body slumped to the balcony floor. Blood pooled from her neck as her lifeless eyes gazed up at the stars.

'Damn, I was too slow,' Atuy said.

'I just killed a child. I killed him...' Tears fell from Veronica's eyes as she spoke.

'Veronica... That was all we could do.' Atuy knelt beside her.

'I tried so hard. I thought I had the solution... But they still died. No... I killed them. I committed an atrocity, a horrendous act that can never be forgiven.'

'You're wrong. We failed. It's that simple. I will carry this with you forever,' Atuy softly spoke.

Veronica turned to him. They shared a silent understanding.

A roar bellowed through the air. They turned to see a massive dark humanoid figure through the veil of night, its gaping jagged mouth steaming.

'Thank you, but right now...'

'Indeed. Let us go, Veronica.'

'Right.'

Unforgiven

Regardless of what happens next,
It won't ever change
It won't ever be washed away
We will carry it forever,
Unforgiven,
Even as the world forgets and moves ever onward,
We will never let go
We will never forgive our sin

Excerpt from *A History of Himiko*
by Goge Fujimoto, 2018

Himiko was one of the first Exorcists known by name. She held both a healing technique and a sealing technique. While her healing technique was powerful and still valued in her descendants, her sealing technique is far more valuable. This technique is simply called Seal and with it, Himiko could seal strong enemies away by using an appropriate vessel. The most notable case is Lucifer, whom Himiko sealed away in Lucifer's human daughter, Satin. From what we can glean, an appropriate vessel is one that contextually fits the target, such as a scroll that contains knowledge about the target or a blood relative of the target. Himiko could strengthen and weaken the seals on all the beings and items that she secured away, along with being able to do the same with other Exorcists' sealing techniques. A good example is how she amplified and improved the sealing technique Cage of the Wailing Beast of the Vance family (which Satin married into, with her husband managing his wife's seal). This is why Satin asked Himiko to be the one to seal Lucifer away and amplify her husband's sealing technique.

In addition, Himiko could use her technique to travel between dimensions, with her being able to open and close the metaphysical seals of reality and travel freely across the planes of existence. None of Himiko's descendants have managed to achieve this to date, but they have developed ways to conjure objects from negative energy that can physically seal people, such as rope coils, holy rope of light and shrine gates.

Chapter 5: Vs The God of Malice and the Angel of Knowledge

05/09/2035 10:15 PM

'Spatial Destruction: Cross Distortion.' Julie released a neat cross that cut through the dark figure of the God of Malice before her.

Its large figure was covered in white characters from countless languages that all spelt out 'hate', 'die' and 'curse.' Julie's attack found purchase. It cut a neat horizontal slice through the God of Malice's body. Yet, its skin healed over the slice, as though her blow had not taken place.

'I can't hurt it?' Julie said as she bit her lip. 'I trained so damn hard. Every day I honed myself, but I... I couldn't save Ethan, or even that poor girl. I'm useless. What was it all for? Why do I have all this power? It's all worthless!'

The God of Malice went to catch her in a large hand. Snapped out of her thoughts, Julie did a quick backward leap to evade. Her leg brushed against the back of the God of Malice's pinkie finger. Waves of agony crashed through Julie. Needles pricked across her body. Hammers rattled within her. Electricity shot up her spine. Julie clenched her teeth as her body hobbled back and forth.

'That was only a nudge... All that agony, from just a touch...'

Yeah, the God of Malice is extremely annoying since it can't physically hurt you, but it can simulate the worst possible pain through physical contact, commented the dark presence within Julie, the Angel of Knowledge, Lucifer.

'Then tell me, how do I destroy this thing?'

The only way to destroy it is to attack from the inside, but that will inflict such immense pain it will probably either drive you insane or kill you from shock. You're not going to be able to beat this guy, so why not let me do it for you? Lucifer's voice offered.

Julie could feel Lucifer's urge to smirk, the wickedness of which brought forth memories of the last time she had not been able to control Lucifer. Lucifer had almost killed her friends. Furthermore, it had only been thanks to her friends that Lucifer did not kill anyone.

'No! I won't let you out! I won't let you hurt anyone ever again!' Julie screamed. Her hands balled into fists.

The God of Malice's backhand struck her. The blow itself did less than nothing. Not even a bruise was left upon Julie. However, the immense agony made Julie fall to her knees. It was as though her skin was ablaze. She felt insects crawling across her nerves and in her eyes. Her organs burst apart and her breath fizzled out.

See? Just this is far too much for you. You can't even hurt it. Why not let me out? Weren't you just saying you're powerless? You're right, you know. You are weak. I am strong though. I have power. Sure, you've tapped into it, but you haven't even reached the first real milestone of potential this power holds.

So, why not pass this battle off to me? Lucifer's voice had become softer, a whisper that tickled the back of Julie's brain. For an instant, an ever so brief instant, Julie considered taking Lucifer's offer. She could rest, simply close her eyes and worry no longer. Though, this moment was fleeting at best, for Julie's friends flashed through her mind.

'Veronica, Atuy, Erica, Jacob, Kyoko, Yuya, Mikoto! I need to protect them. To see their smiles. To... To show Ethan his death wasn't worthless. I refuse. I will never let you hurt anyone ever again! No matter what!' Julie roared as she sprinted toward the God of Malice and leapt into its mouth.

The pain was maddening, unquantifiable, a swirling torture, an agony inexpressible through words or gestures across all cultures. Julie screamed as she unleashed all of her power. She burst through the God of Malice as agony roared through her body. The God of Malice was torn asunder and faded away into nothing.

'I did it...'

Julie smiled as her eyes began to shut. Her body fell toward the ground.

Suddenly Julie's eyes snapped wide open. Lucifer's emerald eyes flicked toward the sky and her body floated upright. She gracefully landed on her feet with a quiet tap. Lucifer pulled Julie's ribbon from her jacket. It blended into the darkness as Lucifer tied back her hair with it.

'Yeah you did, you stupid brat. I have to admit, I was telling the truth. I truly thought the God of Malice would kill you or drive you mad. The fact you not only chose to confront it knowing that, but actually managed to endure it, is truly marvellous. Of all my vessels, you have been the only one to earn my respect. So, have a nice rest, Julie, and don't worry.

Just this once, I'll simply observe out of respect for you,' Lucifer said with a warmth not even she could fully grasp.

'Can we trust you?' Lucifer turned toward Atuy's voice. Veronica accompanied him.

'Oh, hey. It's you two. You sure got strong, but yeah, you can. I always uphold my word. Besides, this night is shaping up to be amusing. I mean, it sucks my favourite, Erica, is already unconscious while that annoying Kujo is still alive. However, that girl with no power is about to have something incredible occur to her. It'll be entertaining to watch.' Lucifer smirked, filled with elation and a childlike sense of curiosity.

'Kyoko? What's going to happen?'

'To be honest, I don't know. That's why I'm going to observe from here. However, I don't recommend you interfere. I think your precious teacher is in far more danger than Kyoko. She's in the city square, alone with Kujo. Though, what you do is up to you guys, so do what you want.' Lucifer shrugged.

Atuy and Veronica shared a glance before they pelted off at full speed.

'Ah, I forgot how good it is to simply watch sometimes. Now, what will happen next? I can hardly wait,' Lucifer giggled as she leapt into the air, sailed onto the roof of a creaking building and perched upon it comfortably. From there she would sit back and observe the humans and their fascinating battle.

Interesting

Old classics,
New sights,
Those once known have since been reborn

How wondrous,
This cardinal night of chaos
In the air,
The sweet ecstasy of battle
On the ground,
The soft touch of blood
Truly,
How wonderous it is to be alive

Decree of the Exorcist Order, 1904

In light of the conflict between Russia and Japan, no Exorcist shall intervene or become involved in the conflicts of non-Exorcists. Any who break this mandate will be tried as traitors, for to bring techniques onto the battlefields of non-Exorcists would be a slaughter. This will stand, regardless of motivation or impact. Demons are the only ones whom Exorcists should turn their blades upon, for an Exorcist to turn their blade on another human is a sin. The only exception is traitors of the Order, which an Exorcist must dispatch with haste and without remorse.

Chapter 6: Vs A Transcendent One

05/09/2035 10:16 PM

Kyoko stood before an oddly normal woman. While she had a plain short sword in her left hand, no bloodlust emanated off her. Very little negative energy around her being. Her eyes were glazed over, her back was slumped and she had her right hand in her jean pocket. Yet, she stood in the middle of a battleground. Kyoko did not allow herself to lower her guard. She kept her hand on the hilt of the sheathed blade at her side.

'Are you Kyoko Nakamura? Hm...' The woman removed a photo from a pocket, lifted it and then turned back to Kyoko. 'Yep, it's definitely you. You're quite pretty. That's a shame. Well, guess I better get to work,' the woman said casually. For a reason beyond her understanding, the woman's words sent a chill down Kyoko's spine.

Kyoko prepared to draw her blade. She was ready for the attack she instinctively perceived coming. However, the woman completely disappeared. Not even her faint negative energy remained. Kyoko side-stepped before she could understand why she had moved. She noticed the tiny cut on her sleeve.

It only grazed the fabric, but if I was just a bit

slower... I would be dead now... This woman... she wants to kill me, but she's different from Yelena. Unlike her, this woman has no bloodlust... She's so cold, so detached. I have to focus, or I will die.

Kyoko had no read on her opponent in the slightest. She could not formulate a plan. All she could do was focus, rely on her senses, and eventually figure out the weakness in her opponent's technique, then she would counterattack. Suddenly, a white glowing coil grasped Kyoko and pulled her back. At the helm of this was Mikoto, she had run from out of the side street and pulled Kyoko to her. The white coil stopped pulling Kyoko when she stood a few metres in front of Mikoto.

'Kyoko! We need to retreat!' Mikoto yelled.

'This woman, she's dangerously strong, right?' Kyoko called out.

'Yes! Her name is June Dakota and she's as strong as a Paladin. Her technique is called Null World. It makes all senses null to her presence, but it also nullifies negative energy, which means techniques used against her will never hit. That's why we need to—' Before Mikoto could finish her sentence, Kyoko pulled her close. A tiny cut formed on Mikoto's neck, not even enough to properly bleed. Kyoko's eyes narrowed. Her body tensed with bloodlust.

'Stay behind me. I will protect you. She won't let us get away. No one else can provide backup to us anyway. With this blade, I'm the only one who can kill her. Right here and now, I will kill her,' Kyoko declared as she drew her blade and held it in front of her as she readied herself for the next strike.

'H-hold on! Surely we don't need to kill—'

'We do. Either she kills us, or I kill her. I will not allow her to kill us, I will kill her instead. It's as simple as that.' Kyoko's mind and body focused on a single purpose, killing June.

I was wrong. The differences between my enemies don't matter. I just need to focus. Focus, focus, focus! Don't overthink it. Just react. Don't trust anything other than my own instinct. To protect the others, I simply have to strike her down. That's all it is.

The world around Kyoko fizzled away. Upon the water was a soft ripple to the right. Kyoko swiftly swung her blade at it. Her blade clashed against another metal before it disappeared.

I feel her presence. I can hit her. I can't get arrogant. I just have to focus. There are only two things I need to do. I'll put everything into them and nothing but them. Protect Mikoto! Kill June! Protect Mikoto! Kill June! Protect Mikoto! Kill June!

05/09/2035 10:20 PM

June Dakota was born into a respected and powerful Exorcist family. They were delighted when they discovered she inherited their most powerful technique. They were ecstatic when she gained strength and became more acclaimed as she slew dozens of powerful demons.

However, June only found boredom in her existence. To her, life was an unending slog of fighting and killing, one without any real satisfaction. It did not matter if her opponents were weak or strong, June only ever felt a ceaseless disinterest as she tore their flesh apart with her sword.

For a brief time, June considered ending her existence out of listless disappointment. That was until she fought Saki Sato, a girl her age who was the only person equal to June. During that fight, June felt cold.

A shiver ran down her neck. When Saki closed in, a single thought occupied June's mind.

I don't want to die.

Saki bested June. She had June at her mercy. Yet, she seemed content with victory and simply walked away. After this fight, June re-evaluated the life she had assumed was worthless. June sought to experience all facets of life, to find why she wanted to live. Friends just tired her out, lovers annoyed her deeply, alcohol was disgusting, drugs were juvenile, and pleasure was out of her reach. As such, her life of boredom continued.

That was until her son was born. June had not intended to get pregnant, but she decided to have her child upon a whim. Her nine months of pregnancy were just as unremarkable to June as any other point in her life. Then, her son was born. As his small beady eyes gazed into June, she could not help but reach out to him. His tiny hand grasped her index finger and he laughed gleefully. For the first time, June smiled.

It's so warm...

She bestowed her son the name Adam and placed him in the centre of her dead universe. June found every instant she spent with Adam truly joyful. They were so precious she felt as though it was too good to be true.

In a way, June was right. Soon her funds from her Exorcist days dwindled. June returned as an assassin, one who would kill humans and demons alike for the right price. She took up the misery of cutting down numerous beings, so she could cherish the refreshing new ways in which Adam presented the world to her. Yet, one person managed to deflect her blows, a person who stood in her way.

Damn it! I wanted this to be over quickly. I promised Adam I'd be home by ten with cake.

June checked the time on her phone.

Ten-twenty... I have time then, time to carefully cut this one down. How should I go about this? She's not just getting lucky. She dodged my first strike and parried in an instant. This must mean she has Universe Perception, that she can perceive anything. So that's what makes her a wildcard. She can instinctively perceive me even when I'm using this technique. Damn, that's annoying. I guess I should speed up and make it harder for her to keep up with me.

June ran far more rapidly than usual and prepared to let out a flurry of attacks that would destroy Kyoko. However, June's instincts screamed at her. She leapt backward as a black speck approached from the corner of her eye. Kyoko swung her blade and neatly lopped off June's right arm. A mist of blood burst from June's shoulder. Her arm hit the ground with a wet thud. Had she not moved, June would have been cleaved in half.

Dammit! How was she able to keep up with me? She wasn't even relying on negative energy. That was all instinct. How the hell did she do that? What is she? She's not human. She's a devil!

June cursed as she tightly gripped the sword in her left hand to bear the pain. She winced.

Damn it! Focus! If I release my technique I die. Just hold it together.

'Y-you hit her,' Mikoto cried out, her eyes drawn to the disembodied arm that sat in a pool of blood.

'Yeah, now I just have to kill her,' Kyoko said coldly. She held her sword squarely in front of herself.

Oh, I get it.

A penny dropped within June's mind. The heat left her body.

Saki Sato was strong, but she just wanted to stop me. She was held back by that. That's why our fight was close. *This girl is only thinking about killing me and protecting her friend. Nothing is holding her back. No doubts, no fear, no hesitation. That's why she's so strong. She's got all that unrestrained power, without any negative energy. Kujo was right. She probably is the only one that could stop him. Hmm... I would like to go home, but... I don't think she'd let me. Damn, I really shouldn't have attacked her friend.*

June smirked at Kyoko's intense face, a demonic face that would hunt June down across the planet. June sped up once more. Her body flashed forward faster than even June had thought she could go. As June attempted to strike, Kyoko calmly thrust her blade forward. It found purchase within June's gut. Blood sputtered from June's mouth as her technique came to a halt.

'Damn... I'm sorry for breaking my promise, Adam...' June smiled before the life left her body.

Kyoko pulled her blade from June with a plume of blood. She watched as the body slumped to the ground. Kyoko silently stood and gazed upon June's corpse. Then she cleaned her blade, sheathed it, and began to walk forward.

'Let's go stop Kujo,' she finally uttered.

'Right,' Mikoto whispered.

Simple

Life is simple
One protects what they love
Ignores what they hate
And kills whatever endangers that which is loved
It is truly simple,

It was a life I have no regrets about
Thank you world,
Being born was worth it

Excerpt from Misaki Sato's diary, 12/05/1895

Our clan's technique, Absolute God Hands, is unmatched by all other techniques. Perhaps that is why I am the first in two hundred years to wield it, but that is not a bad thing. Many of the other clans and families are devoured by pride. The current heiress of the Nakamura is the picture of vanity and arrogance. They have forgotten what our power is for, to protect those who cannot defend themselves from demons and the Exorcists that turn to wickedness, like the wielder of Null World.

I only barely managed to kill her. I had to use Absolute God Hands on my reality to invert my senses and then stabbed the wielder of Null World through the heart with a dagger. Though I won, I was too late to save four other Exorcists from death and because of my ineptitude, an innocent woman was cut down by the Null World user.

This battle was a sobering reminder of why we Exorcists exist, to protect those around us. Titles, pride, and power mean nothing if our comrades and the innocent people around us are killed. That is why I am writing this entry, not merely to note my day and leave a record, but to leave a resolution for the rest of my life and to my descendants. I will live my life to help others. I will never back down from this. As someone with a powerful technique, I will destroy the powerful threats others cannot. My descendants, I ask that you do the same should you become Exorcists, especially if you also come to possess the Absolute God Hands technique, for its power is one of the few techniques that can truly stand against Null World and the demon kings.

Please consider this, but do not feel pressured into it. In truth, I wish that you all have peaceful lives, that you can simply sit back, read books, play shogi, sip tea and brush the fur of a cat lazily every day, that you help the people in the neighbourhood, like when I scared naughty children this morning with my new scar from my right eyebrow to my chin, much to Miss Harada's chagrin.

Chapter 7: Vs
The Master of Now

Caroline's early memories were a haze, filled with images too blurry to properly understand. The only thing Caroline could truly recall from her early years was a distinct tinge of sadness. That sad haze stopped at the first specific memory Caroline had, the appearance of Kujo, the moment when Kujo outstretched his hand to her.

'You poor soul, it is okay. I shall take you with me.' Kujo softly smiled as Caroline grasped his warm hand. From that point on in her memory, everything was crystal clear. It was a cosy paradise, one where her master taught her what life was and why she mattered. That had inspired her, made her want to become just like that master, to bestow unto others what she had been so lucky to receive from Kujo. Then, Kujo changed.

He left the Exorcists without so much as a word and vanished into the shadows. For ten years, Caroline could only wait and hope that her master was alright. All the while she strived to fulfil her goal. She ceaselessly taught so many young Exorcists. Caroline took on the first international class in four years: Kyoko

Nakamura, Ethan Johnson, Veronica Kurlu, Erica Holt, Atuy Honjo, Mikoto Shinatobe, Yuya Kitagawa, Jacob Jillstone and Julie Vance. These nine were the ones Caroline looked upon as her true successors, the ones upon which she wanted to bestow all she knew.

When Kujo reappeared as a terrorist, Caroline vowed to stop him for the sake of her successors. Caroline used Kujo's schemes to make them stronger. She bided her time and formulated a way to properly stop him. She took responsibility, and imparted her students with wisdom and strength.

She smiled at the thought of them, even as the green blade of light pierced her chest. A tearful Kujo held the blade.

'I presume your plan was to use your technique to fully seal the entire city this time,' said Kujo. 'If you continued training in the manner I used to instruct you in, then five months is plenty to gather enough energy to seal a site that size. Clever, but this blade is The Divine Toll. It holds a unique technique born from fifty-seven other techniques I combined. When it pierces negative energy, it negates and destroys all other traces of that negative energy. Sorry, your plan is over, as is your life. I truly am sorry, my dear Caroline.' Kujo pulled the blade out of her chest. A plume of blood followed as Caroline fell onto her back. Despite her plan being crushed, despite her life flickering away, Caroline chuckled.

Weird, I just lost... But I get the feeling they won't lose. In the end, they'll somehow win. Yeah... I have faith... You guys can do it.

05/09/2035 10:24 PM

The sky cracked open. The tiny crack Caroline had sealed tore into a massive hole teeming with unleashed negative energy. Kujo's negative energy spiked, its ripples pulsated out into the surrounding streets. Atuy and Veronica sensed the surge of negative energy and rushed toward the source. The young Exorcists sprinted through the streets of Adelaide. They panted as they spilled from the side street and into the open square. They saw Kujo standing over their master's corpse laying in the streets. Her smile and closed eyes made it almost appear she was asleep in a pleasant dream. Veronica cried out. Tears rolled down Atuy's cheeks as he glared at Kujo.

'You're the one who started all this. I won't ever forgive you!' Atuy put his power into his guardian spirit and thrust it toward Kujo, who simply stood still. The guardian spirit raised its right fist and threw forth a mighty punch, one Kujo caught with his bare hand.

'Inferno Spear of Judgement!' Veronica screamed. A colossal spear of flame hurtled toward Kujo, who completely faded away. The spear plunged into the ground with a deafening crack. Atuy's guardian spirit backed away as Atuy frantically searched for Kujo, only for him to appear behind the two of them.

'Yes, I became a devil for the sake of my goals. I accept your wrath. Caroline, Ethan, Fei, Tina, Tony, June and so many others are dead because of me. But I cannot stop now! I must go on! Look! The portal is already half open! Soon, it will open entirely and this world will change!' Kujo proclaimed before he vanished once more, a feat that did not last long.

Kyoko ran into the square, slid to a halt and immediately slashed at the empty space in front of her.

Kujo reappeared before them, a small scratch upon his face. Kyoko and Kujo stared each other down.

'Atuy! Veronica!' Mikoto rushed into the square. She let out a small breath as she saw Yuya, Jacob and Erica unconscious and flinched at the sight of Caroline. Tears welled as her lip quivered.

'Mikoto, Atuy, Veronica, take our friends and get out of here. I will take care of Kujo,' Kyoko said as she pointed her blade at him.

'Alright,' Mikoto said, wiping away her tears before she used her coil to wrap up Yuya.

'Wait! We should—' Veronica began to say.

'Kyoko, can you win?' Atuy asked firmly.

'Not can. I will win. I promise,' Kyoko said.

'I trust you. Win,' Atuy said as he scooped Erica into his arms and his guardian spirit gently picked up Jacob.

'Right,' Veronica whispered before rushing off with the others, which left only Kujo and Kyoko.

'You truly have become frightening,' said Kujo. 'You are just like Akihiko now. Perhaps even more fearsome, more honed through bloodlust. Perhaps it is fate that you are here at this moment. Caroline's student and Akihiko's descendant standing against me, with Faust's weapon in hand. It is certainly cruel. You poor child.' Kujo shook his head.

'Kujo, I've had enough of your pointless words. I'm ending this battle here.'

'Then I suppose I had best go full force as well. These are my specialised close-combat unified techniques. Only Akihiko could ever keep up with them. Twenty-Thousand Combination: Armour of Desolation and Blade of Crashing Stars.'

Upon Kujo's body appeared bright red samurai armour that shimmered across his body, along with a large, yellow, glimmering cross-shaped blade. Kujo

took the blade in both hands. Kyoko followed suit
with her blade.

They launched towards each other.

You All

I know I failed,
I could not do it myself
Yet,
I can't help but smile
I trust you all
You all are the best there are
Is that bias so wrong?

Excerpt from *The Definitive Guide to Sealing Techniques* by Caroline Copper, 2025

Seals are different from most techniques since they
last after death. Most techniques dispel as soon as
an Exorcist dies, but seals are instilled with negative
energy and are not reliant on the negative energy of
a living Exorcist. This is why some seals have lasted
over a thousand years and others come undone after
a week. The difference comes in the technique and
the way it functions. Some have a simple relationship
where the more negative energy pulled into the seal,
the longer it will last. Others, such as my technique,
work based on a time constraint. I set a time limit and
my technique will seal the target away for that time
limit only, regardless of how much negative energy
I put in or even if I run out of negative energy. The
seal will stand until that time limit is up.

Chapter 8: Vs Toji Kujo

Long ago, a child swung a wooden sword, over and over. She did not relent even as her bruised hand cried for her to cease. As the child swung her sword, a woman walked up to her. The child did not stop swinging. She simply looked out of the corner of her eye at the woman, blonde with porcelain skin and blue eyes, wearing a frilly red with white sleeves and cuffs. The woman held an umbrella aloft and a sheathed sword.

'Hm... So you are the so-called failure of the Nakamura...' the woman finally spoke.

'What do you want? I'm busy right now,' the girl said, still swinging her sword.

'Oh, a feisty one indeed. Yes, I think you will do nicely,' the woman said with a thin smile. The girl scowled.

'For what? I need to keep training. I need to get stronger. I don't have any interest in your schemes, so piss off.' The girl put up her middle finger.

'Schemes? No, no, this is merely a selfish whim of mine. I rather like you, child of the Nakamura clan, a descendant of my old friend who I cherished so deeply. So, here.' The woman held her blade out to the girl. The girl finally stopped her sword swings and stared wordlessly at the sword.

'Go on. Take it.' The woman nodded. The girl slowly approached the sword and placed her hands upon the hilt and sheath. The woman released her grip. The girl staggered under the weight of the sword and then regained herself. She slowly pulled the blade from its sheath with a hiss and her breath stopped.

'A black sword. Isn't this a legendary weapon? That must mean you're that immortal.'

'Indeed. I collaborated in creating this with a friend I made in this very land a long time ago. It never found use, so it has been with me for quite some time. I think it should be put to use. You certainly seem like you could become skilled enough to wield it. So, there. You have it.' The woman chuckled.

'B-b-but, this is the weapon that everyone says can't break. It won't ever rust, chip, or corrode. It can cut through anything and kill immortals. Why are you giving this sword to someone like me?'

'As I said, it is merely a selfish whim. I simply like you and... Hmm... I think you could use it well, I suppose. After all, I get this feeling one day...'

'One day?'

'One day you will be the one to cut the thread of destiny and cut down the immortals that need to slumber so very much.'

'I...'

'After all, you remind me of that world-changing fool.'

Before the girl could ask anything more, the woman was gone.

'Thank you, with this, I can win. I won't stop now.' The girl smiled. Her eyes glistened proudly as she held the blade tightly.

05/09/2035 10:25 PM

Kyoko's blade moved upward. It rushed, seeking to sever Kujo's head. Kujo thrust his armoured wrist at Kyoko's blade. Kyoko tightened her grip. Her blade cut across the surface of Kujo's left arm as she ran forward. She ground her feet to a halt when she was behind Kujo. She did not waste her opportunity. As Kyoko swung her blade, Kujo's Blade of Crushing Stars extended, placing Kyoko on the defensive with no choice but to block the blade as it crackled against Kyoko's sword. Meanwhile, the armour Kyoko had damaged completely repaired itself.

His sword can change its length and extend outward, while his armour can repair itself. Not only that, but his reflexes can easily keep up with mine. He's probably using a combination of Erica's Speed Force and the reflex-enhancing power from that demon Atuy and Veronica fought. This will be difficult... But that doesn't matter. I have to win, no matter what. All I can do is keep attacking until I finally break through.

'Five Hundred Technique Combination: Devouring Earth!' Kujo called out. The earth beneath Kyoko cracked away. Kyoko leapt backward, only for the crumbling ground to chase her back further. As she leapt again, Kujo swung the huge Blade of Crushing Stars in a mighty sweep. Kyoko bent backward in her somersault. The blade harmlessly swung just above her face. Above Kyoko, the sword looked like the night sky, filled with shining stars.

'Three Hundred Fifty Technique Combination: Descending Heaven Javelins!' Spears of light fell from the sky at rapid speed, hurtling toward Kyoko. Kyoko did not evade. She simply stood with her blade raised.

The instant the spears were close enough, Kyoko destroyed them in a flurry of slashes. Kujo did not relent. He charged forward at Kyoko.

'One Hundred Thirty Technique Combination: Thousand Machine Gun Judgment Hellfire Volley!' A barrage of thousands of dark fireballs shot toward Kyoko. She ran at Kujo. As though in a dance, she weaved through each shot. She evaded death by a sliver each time. As Kyoko dodged the final projectile with a clean side-step, Kujo flashed behind her and lunged the Blade of Crushing Stars forward with dizzying speed.

Kyoko rolled forward and struck Kujo's head, but Kujo's helmet batted her blade away. Without a wasted second, Kyoko slashed downward at Kujo's chest and left a large cut within the armour. Kujo responded with a slash at Kyoko's throat. She shifted to her right and then counterattacked. She slashed the same point in Kujo's armour that had not yet finished repairing itself. Kujo's blade grazed her neck. Kyoko's blade completely shattered the armour. It fell to pieces with a clatter across the pavement below them. Kujo soared into the air. His body floated above Kyoko.

'You truly are Akihiko's descendant. No wonder you were able to best June. I will have to overwhelm you with power even Akihiko could not best. Twenty-Thousand Technique Combination: Magus Armour!' Kujo's body was covered by a wide hat, a golden robe and long dark boots. 'He could never best this technique, since it allows me to access a unique ability to activate multiple techniques simultaneously! Triple Cast! Five Hundred Technique Combination: Unending Shock Chain Entrapment! Five Thousand Technique Combination: Blood Homing Sickle Array! Seven Hundred Fifty Technique Combination: Spatial Absolute Destruction!'

Kujo extended his hand. A mass of negative energy

gathered as a ball of power in his palm. At the same time, chains buzzed with electric power and wailed in the air as sickles of blood dripped into existence. Then, all at once, they flew to Kyoko. She did not relent. Kyoko ran forward to Kujo. Without so much as flinching, she swatted away the sickles and chains with her sword. When the ball reached her, its power crackled in the air, she sliced it in half.

'I see. So even that barrage was not enough. Very well, then how about this, the technique that even Paladins cannot beat! Six Thousand Technique Combination: Godspeed Spirit Photography!' Kujo proclaimed.

Kyoko watched very carefully. It was as though, in that single instant, everything turned still. It captured the exact moment Kujo's eyes began to shut. In that instant, that minuscule fraction of a moment, Kyoko flung her scabbard at Kujo's head as she charged forward. The scabbard only blocked Kujo's vision for an instant, yet it was enough for Kyoko to get behind Kujo, leap into the air and raise her sword above her head to strike.

'So, you were able to beat even the strongest version of Spirit Photography! Then, here is everything I have, the accumulation of my soul and resolve. Behold, Kyoko Nakamura! Forty Thousand Technique Combination: Absolute Condensation Spiral Lance!' Kujo's armour faded. Every drop of his power was focused into a lance of all colours, all shades and lights. The lance burst from Kujo's right hand and bore toward Kyoko in silence.

Kyoko's mind was quiet, she knew the only way to win was to destroy this technique. Kyoko did not pause, did not doubt herself. She didn't have time. Kyoko put all of her strength into her sword, trusted herself and thrusted at the lance with all her might. In the next instant, Kyoko fell to the ground with a thud. Winded, she gasped, desperately trying to recover her senses.

Everything's spinning. How am I still alive? Am I still alive? I need to focus. I am still alive. Focus. Focus. Don't let up. I've got to win!

Kyoko forced herself to her feet. Her body ached, but she pushed herself until she finally stood upright.

My sword. It's not in my hands.

Kyoko gritted her teeth.

I'll beat him with my fists if I need to!

Kyoko raised her head and faced Kujo. Her blade was lodged in his chest. Kujo fell to his knees and coughed up blood.

'I... I really won,' Kyoko whispered in a daze 'It's over, Kujo.'

'Yes... I can see that...' Kujo weakly chuckled as he gazed upwards, the crack in the sky slowly began to fill. 'Yet... you surely experienced some of the worst of this world. Why would you not want to change it? Why would you be content to leave it as it is? You have power that could change this cursed world, yet you choose to fight for it, to see it remain without any alterations. Why?' Kyoko felt he was peering into her soul, and that she could see his, twisted, but full of a near bottomless love. For that reason, she answered him with complete honesty.

'This world is the one where the people I love live in, so I will protect it. All I can do is try to make it better step by step. After all, what's the most one person can do? It's better to help them than to cause them pain on some great crusade. All I want is to enjoy my simple days with them until I die,' Kyoko whispered.

'Is that so? You truly are just like Akihiko,' Kujo chuckled weakly through a bloody cough.

'Why are you laughing? None of this is funny. All

this death and killing, all this sadness. I hate it all! I hate that I had to be a part of it. So tell me, just what is so funny? Why does it all have to be like this, dammit?' Kyoko screamed. Tears rolled down her cheeks and onto the ground before Kujo.

'It is not funny. I just finally understand Akihiko's words, now that I have heard them from you. I just had to get killed by an overly compassionate fool like him to get it,' Kujo said, a smile on his blood-drained face.

Kyoko's tears began anew, for as she gazed upon the man, she realised that they could have understood one another, that they could have resolved everything with words.

We didn't have to fight. Caroline... Ethan... The ones I killed... They're all gone forever... Damn it! Damn it all...

Kyoko could only watch Kujo's struggling breaths, as the rain of sorrow continued to fall from her eyes.

Why

Why did we all fight?
Why did we all kill?
Why did we have to lose some?
All that was waiting was this sadness
So then,
Why were we all so desperate to reach this point?
Could we not have come together?
Hey, tell me,
What should I do next?

Excerpt from *The Second Life* by Arthur Silver, 1845

Sure, I helped found the global Exorcist Order in part to help protect everyone across this world, though the work is still incomplete at this point. I can't deny that goal played a part in my reasoning, but the complete truth is nothing that grand. I hate lying about that sort of thing. The truth is, I wanted to make a place that would ensure Kujo and Faust wouldn't be alone in the future, so they will always have people around them long after I pass from this world. They'd be miserable alone. I also wanted to build a world where my family could thrive. My family will live on for generations in a world where our powers are needed and respected. I did this especially for my wife and my eldest daughter. I swear, they are sword addicts. I made my wife a Paladin just to ensure she'd behave, and I'm sure my daughter will follow in her footsteps soon enough. Even if it was to make me suffer, when I die, I'll thank the Administrator for reincarnating me back into this world. Because of him this life is enjoyable. Because of him I had the chance to help my friends and family. Because of him I finally found someone to share my heart with. All I can feel toward this world, to you Administrator, is gratitude.

Chapter 9: Vs The Impudent Apprentice

05/09/2035 10:36 PM

'Amazing! It's been a good few centuries since I've seen a fight like that.' Lucifer chuckled as she stroked her chin.

'Lucy, please refrain from fighting the girl. If you want to fight her, I will have to intervene,' a woman said behind Lucifer.

'Ah, it's you. Relax, I made a promise to those brats not to interfere. You should know best that angels always keep their word. And I thought I told you not to call me Lucy. What a disrespectful little turd you are.' Lucifer scowled, not bothering to turn toward the woman.

'It is my special privilege, as your one and only apprentice. Besides, someone has to keep your arrogance in check, the woman chuckled as she strolled up to Lucifer's side.

'Yeah, that was my mistake. I thought no human would be stupid enough to accept my bargain, or they'd regret it after a mere century. Yet here you still are two thousand years later. No wonder they named stupid bargains after you.'

'How mean. I am not stupid, just an incredibly selfish woman. You can see that in the way people speak of a "Faustian bargain" as a deal made to satisfy a selfish want, one that always has dire consequences.' Fraulein Faust clicked her fingers.

'No, you lost your mind long ago. What kind of child asks an otherworldly being "Please, give me life eternal so I might see days long beyond my own?" Seriously, what the hell was up with you? Even now, it still puzzles me.'

'You simply never asked.'

'I suppose not. I never wanted to understand all that much.' Lucifer shrugged.

'There is nothing much to understand.'

'Is that right? Now you have my curiosity. Tell me, Faust, why did you ask me for immortality?'

'I wondered what life would be like in a hundred years and I happened to see you descend from the heavens that day. So, I followed my whim,' Faust chuckled.

'Seriously? You truly are foolish. No wonder you never tire of this world. You're too damn impulsive.' Lucifer sighed.

'Sometimes, I feel that I made the wrong decision, that I should have just led a normal life and died with the people I loved. Yet, this world always provides something new. A new experience, a new friend and just now, for the first time, a purpose.'

'A purpose? Beyond simply indulging your curiosity? Now that is a change for certain,' Lucifer scoffed.

'Come now, Lucy, you cannot speak like that. After all, you seem rather attached to these children. You allowed little Julie here to use your technique.' Fraulein Faust smiled.

'Think what you wish, foolish apprentice... And I told you not to call me Lucy.'

'You didn't deny it,' Fraulein Faust giggled.

'Shut up! If you were watching—Wait, if you were watching when Julie was using my technique before, why didn't you do anything? Why not intervene in this battle? Kujo's your idiot friend, right?'

'I told him I would neither help nor hinder him. Immortals keep their word too. But I thought I should see this until the end, see him off one final time.'

'He is not dead yet. You could still talk to him before he passes.'

'You have too much faith in me. I am far too selfish for that.' Faust's lips quivered through her hollow chuckle. 'It was a good chat, Lucy. Make sure you switch back to that poor girl soon, alright?' Faust turned and began to walk away.

'Impudent Apprentice.' Lucifer clicked her tongue and closed her eyes. The eyelids lifted to reveal a set of blue eyes. Julie blinked twice. She stood and turned around.

'She's gone,' Julie whispered. A soft droplet fell onto Julie's nose. 'Rain? Here to wash away the battle, I suppose.'

Julie cupped her hands, the water gathered in them as the sky began to weep.

The Next World

Often in the history of human beings, demons were recorded as the most savage and dangerous creatures on the planet. Even early in his life, Toji Kujo found it hard to agree with this assertion.

As a boy, he was trained as a warrior, not to slay demons, but his fellow humans. Honour, power, principles. Those were the reasons he was told war against other humans held meaning. A notion Kujo doubted.

A doubt proven true when his home was burnt to the ground. His family, his friends, his lord. All perished, leaving Kujo alone. He discovered his body was undying. He alone was not able to cross over to the other side.

In the aftermath, Kujo wandered without aim. The lack of purpose in his existence left him numb. After two years, he stumbled upon two starving children. Nanako and Yahiko were orphans who had survived the pillaging of an opposing army, only to lose their parents to disease. Upon seeing their hurt faces and empty eyes, Kujo found his purpose. He saw what he could do with his unending existence. He extended his hand to them and led them forward into a future where they could smile. Kujo continued this for all of his existence. He showed hundreds of poor souls joy as a teacher to students lost and unable to help themselves. However, even though this practice continued all through his life, Kujo's outlook changed in the fateful year of 1625.

He met a girl named Tomoko Nakamura who had run away from her family. The Nakamura family were proficient Exorcists that specialised in the killing of other Exorcists. Tomoko could not accept it and would have rather died than partake in killing humans. Kujo became her master and helped her through the world, though it did not take long for her family to track them down. They surrounded the pair at an isolated shrine. Kujo planned to instantly destroy them using a combination of techniques, but that was derailed when a young man emerged from the shrine. He had spiky hair, relaxed eyes and a thin smile on his lips. He wore a blue coat and a cobalt hakama, with a plain sword in an equally plain scabbard on his waist.

'I know it is none of my business, but I cannot allow you all to attack these two. Please leave them be,' he spoke softly.

He only received laughter and an attack from one of the men. With a breath and a frown, the spiky-haired man drew his blade and swiftly dispatched them. The men of the Nakamura family were strong, but this man easily destroyed each and every one of them, which vexed Kujo as he used no technique or power. He simply was incredibly fast, perceptive, and skilled. Though the thing that awed Kujo the most was the man's expression, that frown devoid of any pride or joy. Most men of such strength would flaunt it, yet this man was hesitant and concerned, so much so that Kujo found himself asking the young man his name and if he would join them.

'My name is... Akihiko Sanda... yeah... that sounds good to me.' Akihiko smiled upon them.

Thus, the three became travel companions for three years. At that time, Kujo wondered about the purpose of people within the world once more. He wondered what he could do, what he was supposed to do and what kind of purpose Akihiko had. Akihiko was an anomaly, one that possessed a strength not observed in the usual realm of humanity. Hence, Kujo concluded Akihiko was brought into the world to change it, as one who possessed power defying the natural order of existence.

'This world is the one where the person I love lives, so I will protect it. All I can do is move through this world step by step. After all, what is the most a single person can do? It is far better to spend my days with her than waste them away. All I want is to enjoy my fleeting life with her until we fade, like a cherry blossom in its final bloom.' Akihiko smiled as he gazed upward at the bright stars above.

Kujo was not able to fully understand Akihiko's reasoning. However, he did understand the feelings

Akihiko and Tomoko shared. Because of that, Kujo did not protest Akihiko's answer. Shortly after, Akihiko and Tomoko were wed. Kujo wished them well and departed the nation he had called home for so long to travel the unfamiliar world. Kujo knew there was something that could be done to change the world. He knew there was something one person could do.

Across the globe, Kujo journeyed. He slowly began to gather knowledge of the world, of the Administrator, and he continued to find new students in the darkest corners of society.

One such student was Arthur. He died of illness not long after they became acquainted, only to reappear in a reincarnated form in 1839 when Kujo happened upon the Exorcist Order, the Order of Western Exorcists that had long protected Europe from demons. He joined hands with Arthur and worked alongside the European Exorcists to expand the Order beyond Europe to incorporate all Exorcists across the world.

In the process, Kujo met another immortal, Fraulein Faust. This woman was a scientist, one who created weapons, devices and even homunculi to allow Exorcists to cut down demons with greater ease. Despite that, Kujo noted she was an oddly compassionate person, one who beseeched the Order to allow her precious homunculi to not be shackled as mere weapons once she realised they held emotions and thoughts. Kujo supported her. He felt a kinship with her and they became true friends.

After thirty years, Arthur died once more, with a smile on his face. His daughter became the Lion Blade Paladin and swore to Kujo that she and her descendants would uphold Arthur's legacy as his comrades. Shortly after this, Fraulein Faust bid Kujo farewell.

'My dear Kujo, I want to see your homeland. Despite my centuries of life, I have seen so little of this vast world,' Faust said.

'Oh? And what will you do there?'

'I will learn about the land, attempt to understand the people who live there and their perspectives. And perhaps... I will be able to create what I seek there.' Kujo distinctly recalled how Fraulein Faust said those words with a quiet smile and distant eyes.

'And what would that be?'

'Well, something to finally break through this world... To offer judgement for someone that escaped it for so long.' These last words before Fraulein Faust's departure made Kujo consider everything he had experienced. It made him consider just what he sought.

Kujo realised he wanted to change the world, but it had not changed despite all of his efforts. The world was within a stagnant void, one where the Administrator did not act. The Administrator did nothing to help anyone. Thus, Kujo resolved to usurp the Administrator, to change the world in the Administrator's place. Kujo fought hard and sacrificed much. He caused an enormous amount of pain and suffered in turn.

'In the end, I failed. I did not change anything even after all the fighting... All those sacrifices... Yet, I understand. It was foolish. I should have listened more. Because I did not... I am sorry... Fei, Tony, Tina, Caroline, everyone,' Kujo spoke into the white void.

'Master!' Caroline's voice silenced Kujo. His head turned to her. She ran up to him.

'It's okay, Master, we understand. You can rest now.' Caroline grasped his hand.

'Yeah! Right, Tina?' Tony chuckled at Kujo's side.

'Right!' Tina said on the other side.

'Thank you, our beloved Master.' Fei bowed before Kujo, smiling.

'You're always so stupid, Kujo. What a moron, right Arthur?' A woman with a mane of red hair remarked with a smirk as she gazed at the man with a blond ponytail beside her.

'That was a little mean of you, Elaine, but my wife's right. Though, that's why everyone loves you,' Arthur said with a chuckle.

'You got lost for a bit there, but you finally found your way back. You finally understood what is most important. I need to thank my descendant for that,' Akihiko chuckled as he placed a hand on Kujo's shoulder.

'Indeed, she truly is a remarkable child. She led you home. So, please be at ease. Everyone is here.' Tomoko smiled as she placed a hand on Kujo's other shoulder.

Kujo saw that in front of him, all of his precious students from across the ages were gathered. Every last one of them smiled upon him.

'Welcome home, Master!' they said in cheerful unison. Kujo could only sheepishly smile.

'I am home. Thank you, my precious ones.'

The Most Precious

Change,
That was the goal
That was what I sought
Yet,
I already had attained something precious
Something already capable of great things
How foolish a being I am
Yet I know,
Those next ones will surely change it
I leave it to them

Excerpt from *The Rejection of Gestalt: The Messiah's Journey* **by Yokoharu Satoimo, 2010**

'So, why are you trying to change the world?' Himiko asked the young man.

'I just want to make a place where you all, my friends, will thrive.'

'What kind of place is that?'

'A place where people are free from gods, where they can overcome their struggles through their own strength and will. A place where everyone can exist, where no one fears being struck down by selfish gods. A place where the strong protect the weak. A place where everyone can suffer, fight, work and smile together.'

'Interesting, I thought you were trying to make an Eden, without war, suffering or pain.'

'What would be the point of that? That would just be a lie, a fantasy not earned by anyone. I want to make a place where people can make Eden with their own hands.'

'You know it won't be easy, right?'

'I know.'

'That people will screw it up time and time again.'

'Probably, but they will make it in the end.'

'Oh? What makes you so sure?'

'Well, I like people. People are amazing, so I'll help everyone and give them blessings to press forward to a new future.'

'Interesting, most people would be so much sadder to create a world that will bring about so much darkness. But you have absolute hope,' Himiko said with a chuckle.

'Of course. Is there anything people cannot achieve?'

'Ordinarily, I would say of course there are things

people can't achieve, but when I'm with you I find myself wavering. Alright, I'll help. I want to see this world of yours.'

Final Chapter: Vs The After Thoughts

10/10/2035 10:30 AM

Erica chuckled. She could not help but find immense amusement in the situation before her, as she stood in the empty corridor, adjacent to the large hall where whispers echoed from.

'Stop that! This isn't funny at all!' Yuya fumed. He crossed his arms and tapped his foot.

'Oh, come on, man. It is pretty funny,' Jacob said with a smile.

'I do understand the irony, but it is certainly not funny! Come on, Atuy, Veronica, help me out.' Yuya turned to them, expecting that as straight-laced and honest people, they would agree with him. Instead, they turned their heads to hide repressed smiles and laughter.

'Yuya, maybe... it is not... so bad,' Julie said with a gulp.

'Not so bad? She's about to piss off the entire Exorcist Order! It's not that I care about them, but this could lead to some immense consequences.' Yuya emanated the energy of a worried spouse. Julie had to hold her breath to prevent laughter from spilling out of her mouth.

'Elder sister, I must agree. This is improper,' Mikoto said to Erica.

Yuya turned to Mikoto only to find himself betrayed. Mikoto held the long sleeve of her shrine maiden gown over her mouth, a not-so-subtle attempt to hide the smile that beamed upon her face.

'Give up, Yuya. We all think it's amusing. Besides, did you think she would show up?' Erica said calmly.

'Right? She was all "Everyone, I need to find someone. It will take some time, but I have to do right by him. Please, wait for me." After saying something that cool, did you honestly think she would stick around for this lame ceremony?' Jacob said.

'Especially since she seemed so disinterested in the ceremony,' Veronica said.

'Indeed. When I mentioned it to her off-handily she called it a waste of time.' Atuy flicked his glasses up.

'Hold on... But... This is for her, right? After Kyoko fought so hard, after she defeated Kujo and saved the world, surely she deserves the rank of Paladin.'

'I think it is a good thing she is not here,' Mikoto said. Everyone turned to her. 'It is a good thing Kyoko does not wish to celebrate or be rewarded for those lives she took. To be honest, Kyoko was incredibly frightening to watch. It was as though she was possessed. It is good to see she hasn't completely changed. She still has the same determination and kindness.' Mikoto's quiet words were accompanied by an equally quiet smile. Erica walked over to Mikoto and ruffled her hair.

'Right, it's a good thing she's on her own path,' Erica said.

'You're right. Sorry.' Yuya looked down at his feet. 'I remember how sick I felt when I took another person's life, how it distorted everything. I was just thinking what this ceremony would do for her, not how she would feel. I wasn't even thinking about our fallen friends. Sorry, everyone.'

Yuya recalled how his chain had burrowed into that man's heart. He recalled the final look of fear on his face. Yuya recalled the funerals of Caroline and Ethan, he shed tears next to Kyoko who stood still, empty, her eyes glazed over.

'It's alright. You were only being kind. Besides, for Ethan and Caroline, all we can do is keep moving. That is what Kyoko is doing. That is what we should do as well,' Julie spoke softly, yet with clear determination.

'Right, we can't erase the past and to forget it. Leaving it behind would be the worst sin we could commit. All we can do is make the future a bit better.' Atuy nodded.

'Yes, we will nurture the next generation and ensure their tomorrow is that bit nicer.' Veronica raised a fist.

'That's what I'm talking about. Let's do that.' Jacob clicked his fingers with a broad smile.

'Yeah, you guys are right. All we can do now is keep moving,' Yuya said with a smile.

'Of course. That is our path in this ceaseless world. Though we might be temporarily separated from her, it is the same path we will surely meet Kyoko on once more,' Erica said.

'Right... Actually, it is kind of funny,' Yuya chuckled as he gazed upward.

'Isn't it? Those stupid old farts don't know how great this generation is. Together we'll find a way to make this world a better place,' Erica said.

Everyone's smiles broke into laughter. For so long, they had been engaged in battle and sorrow, cut away from the joy of their youth. Now they found joy once more.

'That's what I like to hear! Alright, then, I'll help

you all out in Caroline's place,' a tall woman with messy raven hair uttered with a grin. Her leather jacket creased as she fist-pumped. The group was silent as she approached them, her footsteps echoed across the marble floor of the white corridor.

'My apologies for my wife. She's an incurable fool. My name is Kit Sato, her embarrassed husband,' the petite man walking beside the tall woman said as he brushed back his long hazel bangs, they shone under the light from the chandeliers. His navy blue sailor uniform swished in time with him.

'Mister Sato, are you telling me that this woman is Saki Sato? The woman who killed Letrith, the Paladin equally ranked with demon kings?' Mikoto said, her gaze narrowed on Saki.

'You are correct,' Kit said. Saki wrapped her arm around Kit and embraced him.

'Yep, that's me. The great and mighty Saki Sato, the coolest Exorcist with the cutest husband. Pleased to meet ya,' Saki said with a grin and gave double peace signs.

'I see. What a disappointment. You should be ashamed of yourself as an adult.' Mikoto shook her head.

'Sorry, Mikoto can be like that. Be a little nicer, alright? She's offering to help us. Let's hear her out, alright?' Erica said as she patted Mikoto's head.

'Of course, elder sister. My apologies, Paladin Sato,' Mikoto purred.

'All good. I like people with spirit. To be honest, I came here to help Kyoko Nakamura, but she's not here, so I'll help you all out instead.'

'Indeed, we found ourselves fascinated by Kyoko. Though all of you are children worth helping as well,' Kit said.

'How do you want to help us?' Atuy asked as he

pressed his glasses up.

'Simple, we want to help you grow even stronger and give you an idea of how you can change the world. See, Caroline was an old pal and I want to help you in the way I think she would have,' Saki said with a warm smile.

'Why didn't she ever mention you?' Jacob asked as he cocked his head.

'She never mentioned me? But we were best friends! Why wouldn't she bring me up even once?' Saki crossed her arms, her leather jacket squeaking.

'I can't blame her. You're extremely embarrassing.' Kit flicked his hair.

'I would be mad, but you're so cute when you're snarky,' Saki swept Kit into her arms.

'N-not cool at all, m-m-oron,' Kit stuttered through a blush.

'So what do you say?' Saki smirked at the others.

'What did you mean by "an idea of how to change the world"?' Mikoto asked.

'The one thing that stupid geezer Kujo never thought of was to change the world from the inside. Rather than trying to oppose the Administrator and causing so much destruction, why not use your powers to change the world of Exorcists? You guys have already managed to overcome things that stood in the way of generations of Exorcists after all. So, Kit and I will help you get stronger and guide you toward making real change, if you'll allow it.' Saki grinned as she spoke.

'I see... Then, we accept. We won't be helpless anymore. Starting here, we'll work toward making a better future with our own hands. We don't need an Administrator to change it for us. We'll change this world ourselves. Right, everyone?' Julie said, her eyes steadfast.

'Right!' the others said in unison.

'That's what I like to hear. I look forward to working together.' Saki clapped her hands.

10/10/2035 10:35 AM

The blonde woman in the red and white dress could not help but smile as she observed the youngsters, her spirit invigorated by their laughter and conviction.

Keep moving forward for the sake of the dead... Yes, I suppose that is all I can do, my dear Kujo. In the past, I only ever moved forward for myself. That goal of mine was simply to have someone finally judge me, to righteously strike me down. I truly am selfish. After all, I ended up giving the Black Blade away on a mere whim. Yet, that worked rather well, right? With that blade, Kyoko Nakamura was able to finally cut you down. To think my selfish whim ended up helping the young. Perhaps irony is the correct word, that I realise my purpose is to help these youths, purely as a result of my selfishness. The universe certainly has a sense of humour...

'Pardon me, but it appears Kyoko Nakamura will not be appearing,' a man in a suit spoke with a small bow.

'Damn, I really wanted to meet Kyoko. Finally, another sword-Paladin appears, only to be a no show,' said the young woman beside Faust with a sigh. Her red mane of hair fell over her face as her head drooped forward.

'Nothing else to do about it. Sorry, Caoimhe,' Faust said.

'Nah, no problem. Not your fault. Besides, it's good to know we have a Paladin with some guts,' Caoimhe said through a toothy grin.

'Indeed.'

'Caoimhe! I finally found you. Please stop wandering off without me,' a short young man said sharply as he strutted up beside Caoimhe. His wavy hair and long white robe rustled with his exaggerated steps. He sighed and placed his hands on his hips as he stood in front of Caoimhe.

'Welp, that's my call. Back to guard duty. All the best, Faust.' Caoimhe waved to Faust and walked off with the young man in tow, a hand on the large sword that sat at her waist.

'Have a good day, Paladin Silver the Seventh and your Holiness,' said the man in the suit with another bow.

'You're a very well-mannered young man,' Faust chuckled.

'Forgive my impertinence, but I am thirty-five.'

'Oh, that is older for most people, right? Sorry, to me, all of you are so young.'

'Beg your pardon?'

'Never mind, just the ramblings of an old woman. Let us depart.'

'Right away, Paladin Faust.' The man nodded. Fraulein Faust drew out her frilly pink umbrella, followed the man outside and unfurled it.

I will do all I can for you precious buds of youth. I will not stop until Kyoko Nakamura decides it is time to judge me with the Black Blade. Until that moment, I will not stop. I will give them all I have.

Fraulein Faust smiled. Her heels clacked as she finally began to move forward.

10/10/2035 6:05 PM

Rain poured down from the heavens. The bone-chilling wind and the sky held a steadfast grey. A boy of ten or so stood in the rain. His ashen hair was drenched. His listless emerald eyes peered upward. He stood in front of an apartment complex, an old cozy building made from rust-coloured bricks.

Be a good boy and wait for me. I have to do some work for a massive payday. Don't worry. I'll be back by eleven, I promise. I'll bring back that cake you love.

His mother had smiled, the same big smile she always gave him. The boy had found it embarrassing and foolish, but now he found himself missing that playfulness of hers.

'Geez, why can't you show up and give me that stupid smile already? Just where the hell did you go, Mum?' The boy sighed.

He had managed just fine. His mother had hidden money in the apartment, with a note that instructed him to use it should she not return. It was clear from the large sum of money and his mother's disappearance that something was amiss. Or more precisely, the boy found his suspicions about his mother to be confirmed. His mother had worked so little, yet she had never run into issues paying for anything or stressed about bills. In addition, she was always hesitant to talk about work. Just the mention of it was uncomfortable.

'So what? Are you an assassin? Are you even alive?' the boy asked with no expectation of an answer.

A black umbrella obscured his gaze. Holding it was a teenage girl with dark eyes, lacquered hair and a bright smile.

'You're Adam, right? I can tell. You look so much like her,' the girl said with a hand on her chin.

'You know my mum? Let me guess, you were a work acquaintance?'

'My, you are a sharp one. Yes, your mother and I know each other through work,' the girl said.

'What are you doing here?' Adam asked cautiously.

Mum never told me about anyone like this. She's definitely sketchy...

'Well, I came for you. Your mother she... June... will not be back for a long time. She's run into some complications. So, I intend to act as your master and guide you a little,' the girl declared.

Adam understood the scope of her words, knowing what she'd left unsaid. This girl wanted to help him. She truly intended to be a guide to someone who she thought was in need. But Adam knew her words meant that his mother was dead, that this girl had killed her. Adam was not completely certain, though her tense face and fake smile made it clear.

Initially, Adam considered killing her right on the spot. Wrath ran through him for a brief instant. Adam had long braced himself for the possibility his mother would not return.

As a result, Adam's wrath swiftly faded as he gazed upon the girl before him. He saw an immense kindness that he could not bring himself to bring harm to or run from. Instead, he accepted the sadness in his heart and decided to go with her.

'Alright, what's your name?' Tears fell from his face as his mother's smile graced his mind. The girl knelt at his eye level. She placed a hand on his shoulder and gave him a gentle smile.

'My name is Kyoko Nakamura.'

'Where to next?' Adam wiped away his tears.

'I want to take you somewhere I think will be good for you. My friends and I can guide you from there as well. If that sounds okay, pack your things and we'll head out,' Kyoko said with a smile.

'Sure.' Adam nodded. His heart harboured both a hatred that would not fade and an unyielding affection for this strange soft-hearted woman, his master, Kyoko Nakamura.

Milton Keynes UK
Ingram Content Group UK Ltd.
UKHW010756110624
444053UK00004B/267

9 781922 314116